SPECS' WAR

SPECS' WAR

Sara Fraser

This first world edition published in Great Britain 1997 by
SEVERN HOUSE PUBLISHERS LTD of
9–15 High Street, Sutton, Surrey SM1 1DF
First published in the USA 1997 by
SEVERN HOUSE PUBLISHERS INC., of
595 Madison Avenue, New York, NY 10022

Copyright © 1997 by Sara Fraser

British Library Cataloguing in Publication Data
Fraser, Sara, 1937–
    Specs' War
    1. World War, 1939-1945 – Children – Great Britain - Fiction
    1. Title
    823.9'14 [F]

    ISBN 0-7278-5212-4

Typeset by Palimpsest Book Production Limited,
Polmont, Stirlingshire, Scotland.
Printed and bound in Great Britain by
Hartnolls Ltd, Bodmin, Cornwall.

Chapter One

My Mam is getting really fed-up with our cat because it's always having kittens, and she has to put them in a sock and drown them in a bucket of water. She says that somebody should tell our cat that there's a war on and good-quality socks are hard to come by.

Uncle Sid hates our cat because it's his socks that my Mam uses to drown the kittens in. But when he moans to her about it she always tells him, "Moan at the bloody cat, not at me! It's her that keeps on having the kittens."

And then my Mam always forgets to bring the bucket back upstairs after she's drowned the kittens, and Uncle Sid moans because he has to get out of bed and go all the way downstairs to the lav when he wants a pee. Him and my Mam sleeps in the front bedroom. He snores ever so loud and it sounds just like the Jerry bombers when they comes over . . . *Errummm, errummm, errummm, errummm, errummm.*

He's not my uncle really, but my Mam says I've got to call him that. I haven't got a Dad. My Mam says that I did have a Dad once, but I can't remember him. When I ask her about my Dad she gets all angry and tells me, "Ask no questions, and you'll hear no lies."

My sister, Virgy, says that she can remember our Dad.

She's bigger than me though. She's eleven and I'm nearly nine. She says that he run away from us because he didn't like me. She says that if it wasn't for me, our Dad would never have run away. And it was her who started calling me 'Specs', because I have to wear glasses and now everybody in the street calls me 'Specs' as well. Even my Mam.

I don't like our Virgy. She's always telling tales on me and getting me into trouble. She's all tall and skinny and she's got freckles and buck teeth and long ginger plaits. She's horrible!

My Mam says that Uncle Sid is going to be our new Dad someday, when the war is over and then we'll have to call him Dad instead of Uncle Sid. I don't know if I'd like Uncle Sid to be our new Dad really though, because sometimes when he's in a temper he sulks and won't speak for ages, and then my Mam tells him to grow up and stop acting like a silly kid. But he still does it.

One night we was all listening to the man on the wireless telling us about the war and Uncle Sid said, "They ought to put me in charge of the government. This war would have been over long since if I was running the country."

"Yes, it would, Sid," my Mam said, "because you'd have surrendered the very first time that Adolf Hitler shouted at you."

"Surrender?" Uncle Sid said, all fierce. "Surrender? Let me tell you that Sidney Tompkin don't know the meaning of that word."

And my Mam laughed and told him, "Don't pull your face about like that. It makes you look like a mad mouse."

He went off in a sulk then. He's having a sulk with me

2

now, because his budgie flew off and never come back. He had a budgie in a big cage, and he used to spend hours teaching it to talk. He reckoned it could say all sorts of things, like . . . 'Good Morning Sidney' . . . 'Bye Bye Sidney' . . . 'Who's a pretty boy, then?' . . . 'Sidney loves Effie,' and all sorts of daft things like that.

Effie, that's my Mam. Her name's Elfreda, but everybody calls her Effie. But I don't think that the budgie could talk really, it just sounded like it was chirping to me.

I brought Johnny Merry home to hear the budgie talk and we kept saying a lot of rude words to it to see if it would say them back. We didn't half laugh! Our Virgy said that she was going to tell Uncle Sid that we was teaching the budgie bad words.

Then when Virgy went out to the yard, Johnny Merry said, "Let's play dogfights." So we made some paper planes and started having dogfights. I've got some really good paper to make planes with and zeppelins as well. I tear it out of the big Bible that Uncle Sid's got. He reckons its hundreds and hundreds of years old, that Bible. And he reckons it's worth tons and tons of money. He don't know that we uses the paper from it to make our planes though. Johnny Merry says that because it's so big and thick, Uncle Sid will never notice that some of the pages are missing. And anyway he keeps it all wrapped up in the bottom drawer of the dresser and never takes it out. He says that when he's an old man he's going to sell it and he'll get enough money to live on for the rest of his days, 'even unto his dotage'. Yeh, that's what he says, 'the rest of his days even unto his dotage'. He talks funny like that.

But we don't make zeppelins any more because Johnny

Merry says they'm too old-fashioned. So we make Spit-fires and Hurricanes and Meshersmits and Focker Wolves but I couldn't spell them planes properly. I like playing dogfights, but when I play them with Johnny Merry I always have to be the Jerry. Hey, that rhymes, don't it . . . Jerry, Merry . . . Merry, Jerry . . . Jerry the Merry . . . Merry the Jerry . . . Ha ha ha ha!

Anyway, we was playing dogfights, and Johnny Merry said, "Let's get the budgie out and have dogfights with it".

So we bolted the door and window to stop our Virgy coming in and then we let the budgie out. It started flapping about and me and Johnny Merry was dive-bombing it with our planes. I was a Stuka dive-bomber because I can make the best noise. I sound just like a Stuka when I do it. I'm the best in our school at being a Stuka. Johnny Merry was a Nackerjeema, one of them Jap planes. We had to be Jerries and Japs because Spitfires and Hurricanes can't be dive-bombers, can they?

We didn't half have a good dogfight with the budgie. Our Virgy kept on hammering at the window and shouting through the glass at us. She said we was cruel. Then she said she'd tell on us to Uncle Sid. But Johnny Merry said take no notice of her. He said the budgie liked playing with us, and the planes didn't hurt it when they crashed onto it.

The only trouble was that the budgie kept on flying into my Mam's new lace curtains. The old lace curtains set on fire one day and got burned. I got the blame for that. Virgy told my Mam that I'd been playing with matches. But it wasn't me, it was Johnny Merry who was playing with them. But my Mam give me a tanning anyway.

4

We didn't have any curtains for ages after that. Not 'til Uncle Sid come to live with us. My Mam says that they cost a lot of money, but it was worth it to stop nosy buggers looking in to see what we'd got that they hadn't.

Anyway, the budgie kept getting all tangled up in the curtains, so Johnny Merry said let's take the curtains down. We moved the sofa next to the window so that I could climb up on the back of it and get the curtains.

Before I got them down though, I did a tightrope walk along the back of the sofa. I'm a good tightrope walker, you know. I'm the best in our school. Then Johnny Merry pushed the sofa to make me fall off. He don't like to see me doing me tightrope walking. He's jealous because he's no good at it. I fell off and pulled the curtains down off the wall. They got ripped a bit as well.

Then the budgie went up the chimney and all the soot fell down and come out onto the floor. And the budgie never come back. And Johnny Merry run out of the house then.

My Mam went mad when she come home, and gave me a tanning. And Uncle Sid hasn't spoke to me since. He's sulking. He does that a lot.

Chapter Two

Hilda's our lodger, and she sleeps in the attic with Uncle Harold. Uncle Harold is my Mam's brother. Hilda works on munitions, and she always wears trousers and a man's coat and a turban. She wears them all the time, even while she's in bed, my Mam says. Uncle Harold don't work though, because he keeps on having nervous breakdowns.

Uncle Sid says that Uncle Harold has a nervous breakdown every time that someone says the word 'work' to him. Uncle Harold says that he can't help being so sensitive and that it's not his fault that his nerves are so delicate. He says that it's all Granny Smith's fault that he's like he is.

Granny Smith is my Mam's Mam, and she sleeps in our back bedroom with me and Virgy. She goes a bit funny in the head now and again, but she's all right for most of the time. A bit miserable though.

My Mam says that she wishes Granny Smith really was a sour apple, and then she could put her into a barrel and store her away until she got sweeter. I laughed when my Mam said that. You get it don't you? There's a Granny Smith apple, and there's our Granny Smith. Ha ha ha ha! My Mam's funny sometimes the things she comes out with. Uncle Sid says that my Mam ought to be on the wireless with all the other comics. But he only says that when she's been having a row with him.

Anyway, Uncle Harold told me that it's Granny Smith who gives him his nervous breakdowns, because of what she does when the Jerry bombers comes over. When the bombers comes over we all gets into the pantry under the stairs. It's ever so good. We has a lighted candle, and a bottle of pop and we sings and tells jokes. Unless Miss Freeman is there, because she comes in with us sometimes. She takes turns to go under different peoples' stairs when the Jerries comes over. It's not so good when she comes because she's very religious and she don't like to hear jokes and songs. She only likes to pray.

Uncle Sid says that she's a bloody Bible punching Old Maid, and he says that what she needs is a bloody good seeing to from a real man. She wouldn't bother about going to church then. She'd only want to get into bed and have some more 'how's your father'.

When he says that my Mam always tells him, "Well, if it's a real man she needs, it's no good her looking for him in this bloody pantry, is it? You and Harold couldn't fill a midget's jock-strap between you." I dunno what she means when she says that, but Hilda always laughs.

Well, sometimes when the Jerry bombers comes over Granny Smith has one of her funny turns. And what she does is she runs out into the back garden with a lighted candle so that she can see the Jerries, and she tells them off for waking her up. She walks up and down waving the candle about and shouting, "Come down here where I can see you, you Jerry buggers! I'll give you such a smack in the chops if I gets me hands on you. Sod off

8

to your own end of the street, and let decent folks get their rest."

And every time Granny Smith does this, Uncle Harold has one of his nervous breakdowns, because he reckons that the Jerries can see the candle and they'll aim their bombs at it, and then we'll all be blown to smithereens. He lies on the pantry floor with his hands on his head, and keeps on shouting, "Will somebody please shoot that silly old cow! Will somebody please shoot that silly old cow! Will somebody please shoot that silly old cow!"

Uncle Sid won't never go out and fetch Granny Smith in. He always says that it's too cold outside, and if the bomb drops he wants to be sitting all warm and cosy for his last moment on God's Good Earth. He don't want to be shivering with the cold when he meets his Maker, because he doesn't want God to think that he's shivering because he's scared of the bombers. Uncle Sid says that he's scared of nothing.

I told you he talks funny, didn't I?

So what happens then is my Mam and Hilda always goes down the garden and they blows the candle out, and they stays out there with Granny Smith if she wants to keep on shouting at the Jerries.

Uncle Harold always says that they ought to stop Granny Smith from shouting at the Jerries as well. Because if the Jerries hears her they might get mad and drop their bombs even if they can't see the candle anymore. But my Mam always tells him not to talk so daft. She says, "How are the bloody Jerries going to hear the poor old soul shouting at them above the noise of thier engines? Have a bit of sense, will you, Harold."

Then her and Hilda looks at each other and laugh.

9

When the Jerries have gone, Uncle Sid always says that it's a bloody good job for them that he aren't still a night-fighter pilot. Because they'd be sitting ducks for an expert shot like he is. He says that in his squadron he was known as Hawkeye, because he never ever missed his target. He says that to be a night-fighter pilot you have to eat lots and lots of carrots, then you can see in the dark. He says that he had to stop being a night-fighter pilot himself, because eating all those carrots turned his skin yellow and made him glow in the dark so the Jerries were able to see him coming and they used to run away before he could catch them.

Me Mam and Hilda laughs when he says that, and tells him that he could always go and be a night-fighter pilot for the Japanese Airforce. But they shouldn't laugh at him, should they. It's not his fault that the carrots turned his skin yellow, is it . . .

Uncle Sid don't like the Yanks. He says they're all bigheads, and they're all mouth and trousers. My Mam used to like the Yanks. She was always talking to them. But after Uncle Sid saw her talking to a Yank one day they had a big row, and she don't talk to them now. I don't think that she likes them any more.

My Mam and Johnny Merry's big sister, Doreen, had a row one day in the street, and my Mam told Doreen that she was nothing but a Yank's tart. And Doreen told my Mam that she was a bleedin' jealous old cow who was too bleedin' long in the tooth to find a Yank who'd want to get between her bleedin' legs. She swears a lot, Doreen does. She said that my Mam had chucked herself at half the bleedin' Yank army, and that none of them had even tried to bleedin' well catch her . . .

10

Then my Mam told Doreen that everybody knew that it was her who chucked herself at the Yanks and that they'd all caught her easy enough, and they caught something else as well that they hadn't bargained for. Then my Mam and Doreen started fighting, and some men had to run out from the pub and stop them.

Johnny Merry says that his big sister Doreen has a Doo with her boyfriend every night. He spies on them, and he's promised to let me come and spy on them as well next week. I've known for a long time what having a Doo is, because I used to watch our cat and Mrs James's black tom having a Doo. I don't think I'd like having a Doo though, because they never looked as if they was liking it.

He's a Yank, Doreen's boyfriend is. He's a Blackie as well. When he laughs his teeth are ever so big and white. Uncle Sid says that's because the Blackies are all cannibals and they need big teeth to crunch the bones up with.

When I asked Doreen's boyfriend if it was true what Uncle Sid had said, he looked ever so fierce and he told me to tell Uncle Sid that the next time he met him he'd crunch his goddam head up.

When I told Uncle Sid, he said, "Phoooo, I'd like to see him try! I could make mincemeat out of him!" Uncle Sid says he's hoping to meet Doreen's boyfriend out in the street one day, then he'll show him what's what. But whenever Doreen's boyfriend comes down our street Uncle Sid always seems to be somewhere else.

My Mam says it's disgusting the way Johnny Merry's big sister carries on. 'Dorrie No Drawers', my Mam calls her, and she says that she's anybody's for a stick of gum, especially if it's Tutti Frutti. I wish I had a stick of gum to chew now. Johnny Merry has always got sticks of gum. He pinches them out of Doreen's handbag. I wish my Mam had a Yank boyfriend instead of Uncle Sid. Even if he was a cannibal, I'd have lots of chewing gum then.

I went to the pictures this morning. The Saturday Morning Club it's called. It only costs a tanner, and there's the serial and cartoons and a big picture. Sometimes there's a little picture as well. We have to sing though before the pictures start.

There's all different songs, the words comes on the screen and the man stands with a long stick and points to the words you have to sing. There's one song that we have every week. It's this one:

> *We come along on Saturday morning*
> *Greeting everybody with a smile.*
> *We come along on Saturday morning*
> *Knowing it's well worth while.*
> *As members of the Gee Bee club*
> *We all intend to be*
> *Good citizens when we grow up*
> *And champions of the free*
> *We come along, on Saturday morning . . .*

We sings that one about ten times I reckon before the man lets us stop.

We all shouts and whistles and cheers and boos when it's a good picture, and sometimes we all stamps our feet together. It don't half make a racket. And then the man comes down and tells us off and the picture stops until we're quiet. The man's got a wooden leg. Johnny Merry says that his real leg was blown off in the last war. And he

12

walks ever so funny. We calls him 'Dot and Carry One' and when he comes down to tell us off Johnny Merry always cheeks him and then the man chases him, but he can't catch him because he's only got one leg to run on, hasn't he?

It only costs me and Johnny Merry a tanner for both of us to get in. One of us pays to get in, then runs quick down to the bottom lavs and opens the window. One week I hides outside and climbs in, and the next week Johnny Merry does. We lets some of the other kids climb in as well, but they has to pay us thruppence, else we don't let them.

We spends the money on Kayli, and licorish root. You can get a lot of Kayli for a tanner. I was in the shop the other day and that posh kid who lives at the top end of our street come in, and he asked for a quarter of Lemon Sherbet Powder. And do you know what it was? It was Kayli. I never knew it had a posh name like that.

That posh kid, his name is Aubrey. That's a daft name. It sounds like a girl's. His other name is Jones-Evans. Yeh, it's two names really. Jones is one, and Evans is the other. I wonder why his Mam and Dad wanted two names instead of just one? It's more trouble to write two names I should think.

Mr Jones-Evans has got a car and Mrs Jones-Evans always wears a fur coat. Even when the sun's boiling down she wears it. My Mam says that Mrs Jones-Evans is so stuck up that she even wears her fur coat when she goes to the lav. Our lav's down the bottom of the yard, and it arn't half cold in the winter. I wish I had a fur coat to put on when I have to go to the lav.

Uncle Sid says that they're nothing but bloody jumped

13

up Taffy pit props. And he says that they keeps their coal in the bath.

We haven't got a bath in our house. But my Mam gets the tin bath out from the coalhouse and puts it in front of the fire and we have a bath in that. Not very often though, because Uncle Sid reckons that having a bath is bad for you. He says that the water washes the natural oils from your skin and makes it easier for you to catch a cold. He says that a man where he works used to have a bath every day, and the man caught pneumonia and died because all the natural oils had been washed off his skin.

Uncle Sid never has a bath, but he washes his feet sometimes. His feet don't half smell when he takes his boots off. My Mam always says that the stink could kill a fly at 50 paces. She says his feet smells just like rotten fish. When she says that Uncle Sid always says that he knows something else that stinks like rotten fish as well, and then my Mam always goes mad and shouts at him. She says that the stink never seems to put him off, does it. She only wishes that it did and then she could get a decent night's sleep for once.

I wonder why they always goes on about rotten fish? If I remember I'll ask Johnny Merry about it tomorrow . . .

Chapter Three

The Yellow Van come and took Mrs Gibbs away again today. She was running up and down the Hill with no clothes on. She was showing all her tits and everything. She's always doing that. Me and Johnny Merry and the rest of the kids was watching her run up and down, and one kid got scared and threw a stone at her when she come close to him. Then a man come out of his house with a blanket and wrapped it round her. And then some more people come out of their houses, and one man shouted at us kids, "Bugger off down to your own end and mind your own business."

And Johnny Merry cheeked him, and then the man chased him but he couldn't catch him. Johnny Merry arn't half a good runner. He's the best runner in our school.

I hope Mrs Gibbs comes back soon because me and Johnny Merry likes to go and listen to her shouting when it's the dark nights. She don't put any lights on in her house, and she keeps on talking and shouting and there's nobody else there. It's ever so spooky. Johnny Merry creeps right up to her windows, and sometimes he calls to her, and then she shouts, "Is that you, Albert? Is that you, son? Have you come back to me? Where are you, son? Where are you, Darlin'?"

Then she comes to look out of the windows. When she looks out, Johnny Merry creeps to another window and calls again, and then she comes to that one as well. One night she didn't come to the window to look out though. She come running out of the door and tried to grab hold of Johnny Merry. He didn't half scream loud. It nearly fritted him to death . . . and me as well. We didn't go back up there for ages.

I told my Mam about Johnny Merry doing that and she went mad. She said that Johnny Merry was a wicked little bugger, and that if she ever caught us creeping around Mrs Gibbs house she'd tan the skin off our backsides. My Mam said that Mrs Gibbs' son had been lost at sea. A Jerry U-boat had torpedoed him . . . and that was what sent Mrs Gibbs mad.

There's a lot of mad people in our town, you know. There's Tick-Tock the Clockwork Man, and Dirty Gertie, and the Stargazer, and Mad Jack, and Bertie Shellshock, and Flossie Wristwatch, and a lot more as well. We don't half have a lot of fun with them.

I like it when Flossie Wristwatch comes up our street. She's ever so fat and she can't walk very well. Johnny Merry keeps on running up to her and asking her the time. And she always tells him, "I can't tell you because I haven't got me wristwatch on. But I think it's half past midnight."

And then we all takes turns to run up and ask her the time and she keeps on telling us the same thing, and then she always loses her temper and she starts to pick up the gravel and throw it at us. One day she picked up a piece of wood that had dropped off Mr Lambert's woodcart and she threw it at Johnny Merry, and it hit him and cut his head open. When I told my Mam about it, she said, "Bloody good job. It serves the wicked little bugger right. I wish she'd bloody well killed him, and then we'd all get a bit of peace . . ."

None of the grown ups in our street likes Johnny Merry, you know. But I likes him because we have such a lot of fun. He'll do anything you dare him to.

Sometimes there's a man comes round the street selling dead rabbits. Me and Johnny Merry always watches to see who buys them, and then we goes and asks for the skins. We takes the skins down town to the Rag and Bone yard. You get tuppence for a skin. The Rag and Bone man is called Charlie, and he's got a wife called Daisy and a big son called Filthy Cyril. They aren't half dirty. And they don't half stink. Charlie always wears a big cap and a big overcoat, and he's got a lot of old medals pinned all over the front of his coat. And Filthy Cyril always wears a trilby hat and no shirt, only his jacket and vest. Filthy Cyril don't wear any socks either, but his feet are so dirty that it looks as if he's wearing black socks anyway. You have to get ever so close to see that he's got no socks on really. Daisy always wears an old fur coat and a big hat with flowers on it.

My Mam says that Daisy and Mrs Jones-Evans are birds of a feather. They're both silly cows who thinks that they're Lady Muck swanking round the town in their fur coats. She says the only difference between them is that Daisy is better looking and has got more style. I dunno what style means though, and when I ask my Mam she always tells me that I'll understand when I'm grown up. There arn't half a lot of things that I'll understand when I'm grown up, arn't there!

17

Charlie and Daisy and Filthy Cyril goes all round the town with two big prams to collect rags and bones. When Charlie gets tired he sits in the pram and makes Daisy push him. My Mam says that Filthy Cyril is simple-minded, but Uncle Sid says that Filthy Cyril arn't simple-minded enough to go off and fight in the war like the rest of the blokes of his age has to. Uncle Sid reckons that Filthy Cyril is as artful as a cage full of monkeys.

I know a man down town who's got a big monkey. He lives by himself because his wife run off with a Chinaman. He's named Mr Cook and he's got a lady monkey. He keeps it in a big cage in his house. He let me and Johnny Merry go and see it once. Johnny Merry poked his finger through the bars and the monkey bit it and made it bleed. Mr Cook told Johnny Merry off for tormenting the monkey and told us to bugger off. When we was out in the yard again Johnny Merry shouted, "Thank you for letting us see your wife, Mr Cook."

Some women in the washhouse didn't half laugh, and Mr Cook went mad. He come roaring out of his house and we didn't half have to run fast to get away from him.

When I told my Mam what Johnny Merry had shouted, she laughed as well and said, "There's many a true word spoken in jest."

I'd like to have a monkey. I asked my Mam if I could have one and she said no, because she wouldn't be able to tell the difference between us. What a daft thing to say . . .

Tarzan's got a monkey. It's called Cheetah. I've seen all the Tarzan pictures. They arn't half good. But I like Flash Gordon best. When he fights the Emperor Ming and shoots his raygun we all cheers and shouts. The only trouble is that Flash Gordon is a serial, and whenever it gets really good, the serial stops and you have to wait 'til next week to see what happens. We play at Flash Gordon sometimes, and sometimes we play at Tarzan.

One time we was playing Tarzan and we was swinging on Miss Freeman's lilac tree. The one that's in her back garden. We can only play in her back garden when she's gone to work, because when she's at home she always chases us off.

Aubrey, the posh kid, was looking out of the window in his house watching us play. Then he come round a bit later on to tell us that he'd told his Mam on us, and his Mam said we'd got to take our rope down off the tree and get out of Miss Freeman's garden straight away. Aubrey said that if we didn't then his Mam was going to fetch a policeman to us. He always says policeman, not copper, because he's posh.

Me and Johnny Merry got hold of him and we tied him up on the rope and started to give him a swing. We was pushing him really high and he was crying and screaming for his Mam to come and get us. Then the branch broke and he fell down, and his Mam come running round the corner shouting, "You've killed him! You've killed my precious darling. You've killed him!"

He was crying and screaming and me and Johnny Merry was laughing so much that we couldn't run fast, and his Mam didn't half clout us.

Then she went to tell my Mam what we'd done to Aubrey, and my Mam told her to bugger off. My Mam said that Aubrey was nothing but a little pansy and that he was spoilt to death. She told Mrs Jones-Evans that she ought to let Aubrey out to play with the other kids and stop wrapping him up in cottonwool, and then he wouldn't be such a sneaky, whining little pansy.

Mrs Jones-Evans said that she was going to fetch a policeman to my Mam, and my Mam said that Mrs Jones-Evans could fetch the whole bloody British police force if she wanted, and the army, navy and airforce as well, because my Mam didn't give a toss for any of them.

Mrs Jones-Evans went off shouting and bawling, but nobody come to our house. I reckon that the coppers are fritted of my Mam, you know.

But then Miss Freeman come home from work, and she come round and told my Mam that I'd broke her lilac tree. My Mam always feels sorry for Miss Freeman because she says that she's a pitiful Old Maid, and so she went mad then, and she didn't half give me a tanning. I couldn't sit down for ages because my bum was so sore. It arn't fair though, is it. Because Johnny Merry never got a tanning for breaking Miss Freeman's lilac tree. He never gets tanned, Johnny Merry don't . . .

Chapter Four

When I was small my Mam always told me that she found
me under a gooseberry bush. I didn't know where babbies
come from then. But I know now. They grow in eggs in
their Mam's tummies. And it's their Dads who puts the
eggs there when they have a Doo. And when they'm big
enough the babbies comes out of their eggs and out from
their Mam's bellybuttons.

I've just thought of something. I bet that my Mam only
said that she found me under a gooseberry bush for a joke.
Ha ha ha ha ha!

When Uncle Sid is trying to talk posh he calls people
'Good Eggs' and 'Bad Eggs'. My Mam says that he
makes a right prat of himself when he tries to talk posh.

Mr Jones-Evans talks very posh. My Mam says that
he speaks the real King's English, even if he is a bloody
Welshman. I don't reckon that he is Welsh anyway, nor
Aubrey, nor Mrs Jones-Evans, because we've got two
Welsh kids at our school and they talks ever so funny.
But they're tough, so me and Johnny Merry are friends
with them.

The nurse come to our school today. She looks at us
to see if we've got pigs in our hair. Only she don't call
them pigs, she calls them lice. Nearly all the kids has got

21

them. I haven't though, because my Mam gets a pig comb and combs my hair nearly every night. She puts a piece of newspaper on the floor and I have to bend over while she combs me hair and all the pigs fall down onto the paper, and then she screws it up and throws it on the fire. She says that if you listen very carefully you can hear the pigs squealing just before the fire makes them go pop. I always listen very carefully but I've never heard them squealing.

Johnny Merry has though. He's heard them stacks of times. He told me that one night his big sister combed some pigs out of her hair and threw them on the fire, and they squealed so loud that the neighbours come knocking on the door because they thought that somebody was being murdered.

Nobody ever gets murdered round here, worse luck, because I'd like to see a real detective. I've seen a detective on the pictures lots of times, but I've never seen a real one. Some of the coppers down town don't wear their uniforms, and my Mam says that they're detectives, but I don't reckon they're proper ones, because they don't shoot any guns like the detectives on the pictures do. And anyway, they don't talk like the Yanks talk. All the detectives I've seen on the pictures talk like the Yanks talk.

Once me and Johnny Merry was in Terry Murtagh's house when the coppers come there. They come and knocked on the door and Terry's Dad was lying on the sofa. He's only got one eye, Terry's Dad has. He wears a pink patch over the one that he hasn't got. Terry let them in and they come into the room and said to Terry's Dad, "You know why we're here, don't you, Ivor? You've been breaking open the gas meter again, haven't you? The gas man told us what you'd done."

Terry's Dad jumped up and shouted at us kids, "You thievin' little bastards! I welcome you into my home and this is how you repay me, by robbing my gas meter. You thievin' little bastards!"

The coppers laughed, and one of them said, "Nice try, Ivor. Nice try, but it won't wash."

"Don't you dare call me a thief!" Terry's Dad told them. "I lost this eye fighting for my King and country."

"You're a liar," the copper told him. "You never had that eye to start with."

They dragged him off to jail then, and Terry's Mam come in just as they was all going out. One of the coppers told her, "Try not to upset yourself too much, my duck. He shouldn't get more than twelve months."

"I hope the bugger gets twelve years," she told him. Me and Johnny Merry went back home then.

My Mam says that it's a shame for Terry Murtagh. She says that his Dad's no good and ought to be locked up for life for the way he treats his missis and kids.

Mrs Murtagh's always got black eyes. Last year she had her arm and leg in plaster as well. Terry said that his Dad come home drunk and chased his Mam upstairs with the chopper and she jumped out of the upstairs window.

Johnny Merry said, "Tell her to use a parachute next time and then she won't hurt herself."

My Mam went mad when I told her what Johnny Merry had said, and she called him all sorts of names. But I don't know why she did that, because I thought it was a good idea for Terry's Mam to use a parachute. So did Terry.

Terry's got lots of brothers and sisters. They has to

23

drink their tea out of jam jars because they haven't got any cups and saucers in their house. Terry says that they used to have cups and saucers in their house but his Dad used to chuck them at the kids and they all got bust.

Terry says that when they've got a bag of chips for their dinner, his Dad chucks the bag of chips onto the table and all the kids have to line up against the wall. Then his Dad blows his whistle and the kids have to run and snatch as many chips as they can get hold of for their dinners. Terry says that when he was small he never ate for years because he couldn't reach up onto the tabletop. His arms weren't long enough. He says he's got one brother who's never ate anything in his life because he's deaf and he can't hear the whistle, so by the time he sees the other kids run and snatch the chips it's too late for him to get any because they've all gone. It's good in Terry's house when his Dad is in the pub though. His Mam don't care what the kids do, and we play all sorts of good games.

We was playing at camping one night in the dark. We had a sheet that we got from Terry's Dad's bed and we made a tent in the back yard, and we had a candle. We was telling ghost stories and when it was Johnny Merry's turn he told us about Frankenstein. I saw a picture about him. He's a monster who's made out of dead people. Johnny Merry is the best ghost storyteller in our school. He's got a book with lots of stories about ghosts and monsters.

He was just telling us about Frankenstein walking all stiff, and killing people with a great big knife, and Tony Jarvis screamed, and when I looked up I saw this great big shadow coming over the tent just like it was in the picture, and I screamed too.

"It's the monster!"

Then everybody starting screaming and the monster roared, and a chopper come down through the top of the tent and nearly hit us. We all run out screaming and shouting, and then the monster fell down onto the tent and was lying on the ground roaring. And Terry's Mam come running out into the yard screaming, "Ivor, you drunken mad bastard, you could have killed one of them kids!"

When I run home and told my Mam that Terry's Dad had tried to kill us with a chopper she went mad, and give me a good tanning because she'd told me not to go to Terry Murtagh's house to play.

Johnny Merry never got a tanning though . . . it's not fair! He never gets a tanning!

When I told my Mam that Johnny Merry never gets a tanning, she said that that was because nobody loved him enough to care what he did and correct him when he did wrong. She said that if she didn't love me, then she'd never bother to give me a tanning. Well, I reckon that giving me a tanning is a funny way to love me.

Chapter Five

Frankie Savin come home on leave from the army today. He's a paratrooper. His Mam and Dad live next door to us. I like Frankie, he always brings me some empty bullet cases when he comes home. And he shows me how to do unarmed combat, and how to shoot guns, and how to jump out of a plane with a parachute. Frankie's ever so tough and brave. He's a lot tougher and braver than that Yank, Doreen Merry's boyfriend.

Frankie's big brother, Colin, was in the army as well. But he got killed in the desert. His Mam didn't half cry when the postman brought the telegram to tell her that Colin had been killed.

Uncle Sid said that Colin had died for King and country, and that it was an honour to do that. My Mam didn't half shout at him when he said that. She said if he thought it was such an honour to get your head shot off, then why didn't he go and fight for the bloody King and country himself?

Uncle Sid said that he'd done more than his bit. And he could tell her stories about fighting that would make her hair stand on end, but he wasn't allowed to talk about what he'd done because of the Official Secrets Act.

My Mam said that the only regiment he'd ever been in

was the bloody 'Royal Standbacks'. And that the nearest he'd ever been to action was when a boiled egg exploded in the saucepan. She said that the only Jerries he'd ever seen was on the news at the pictures.

Uncle Sid looked all upset then and he sulked and wouldn't speak to her for ages. Like he's sulking with me because of the budgie. I hope he speaks to me again soon though, because I want to ask him about the Royal Standbacks.

I asked Frankie Savin about them, and he said that they was the most popular regiment in the British Empire. He said everybody wanted to join them. Then he laughed and wouldn't tell me anymore about them. He said I'd have to wait until I grew up and then maybe I'd be able to join them meself.

I'm going to be a paratrooper though, like Frankie is. He wears a red beret, and he lets me wear it sometimes. It don't half look good.

Me and Johnny Merry sometimes goes and watches the Home Guards down the fields by the railway tunnel. They creep about, sneaking up on each other and shooting their guns. They don't shoot real bullets though, only pretend ones.

Mr Jones-Evans is in the Home Guards. He's a Captain. I know he's a Captain because whenever Mrs Jones-Evans talks about him she always says, "My husband, Captain Idris Jones-Evans."

My Mam says that he's another of the Royal Standbacks. But he can't be in them, can he, because he's in the Home Guards. Uncle Harold told me that he joined the Home Guards, but when the sergeant kept on shouting at him he had a nervous breakdown so he had to leave them.

Uncle Sid laughed all nasty-like when he heard Uncle Harold tell me that. "Oh yes, Harold, I knows all about your military service. When you joined the Home Guard it was called the Local Defence Volunteers, wasn't it? The LDV. Their regimental motto was 'Look, Duck and Vanish', and that's just what they would have done if they'd ever seen a Jerry."

And Hilda said she didn't know what he was sneering and laughing at, he should just look at his own war record, because that motto suited him to perfection. Uncle Sid went off in a sulk then.

Us kids goes over the fields sometimes looking for Jerry paratroopers. Johnny Merry says that we'll know them when we see them because they'll be dressed like nuns, and they'll have tommy-guns. When we goes to look for them we all wears our helmets, and we takes our guns with us. They aren't real guns, but Johnny Merry says that the Jerries won't know the difference.

We haven't found any Jerries yet, but one day when the snow was on the ground we saw this soldier laying down behind a hedge. He looked ever so scruffy, and he was shivering and his teeth was rattling. When he saw us he run away. We told the Home Guards and they went to look for him. One of them said that he was a deserter.

I told my Mam about it, and she said, "Poor bugger! He's some pitiful woman's son." But Uncle Sid said that if they caught him he ought to be put up against a wall and shot.

My Mam just clucked her tongue and shook her head then stared at the ceiling for a long time. I looked up at the ceiling to see what she was looking at, but I couldn't see anything.

Fatty Polson's Dad is always running away from the army. My Mam says that he does it so regular you could set your clocks by him. We always know when he comes home because Fatty Polson tells us that his Dad is hiding down in the coal cellar again.

When the Redcaps comes to fetch him, all the neighbours comes out to watch. Mrs Masters says it's better than going to the pictures, the show that Mrs Polson puts on. Mrs Masters says that if Mrs Polson went to Hollywood she'd make a fortune as a tragedy actress. Mrs Polson's ever so big and fat, and Mr Polson's the same. Mrs Masters says that they ought to be named Tweedledum and Tweedledee.

Mrs Masters lives on the other side of our house. I like her because she's always smiling and laughing. She always calls me Chucky Face and pats me on the cheek when she sees me, and asks me how me love life is. When I ask her what a love life is, she just laughs and tells me that I'll find out when I start erecting the Blackpool Tower. I asked my Mam what Mrs Masters meant, because I don't know what erecting means, but my Mam wouldn't tell me. She said I'd find out when I was grown up. So I asked Johnny Merry, but he didn't know either.

Last time the Redcaps come to fetch Mr Polson it was raining. But everybody still come out to watch. When the Redcaps come out of the cellar with Mr Polson they was all covered in coal dust, and when they come out into the rain the black was running all over their faces and clothes and their white belts. They was all shouting and swearing about it.

Then Mr Polson lay down on the road and he wouldn't

30

get up. So they had to go to the ARP post at the top of the street and get a stretcher to put him on. But he's so big and fat that they couldn't hardly manage to lift him, and they only walked a couple of steps and they had to put him down again. All the neighbours was cheering and clapping, and Mr Polson was grinning all over his face.

Then the Redcaps went and got the Co-op horse and cart from the stables down the bottom of our street, and they put Mr Polson on the cart.

Then Mrs Polson lay down on the road in front of the horse, and she tried to make Fatty Polson lie down with her as well. Fatty Polson wouldn't lie down though, he came to hide behind Mrs Masters. Mrs Polson was shouting, "Don't take my darling husband from me. Don't take him to his death! Let him live! Let him live. Take me instead and kill me. Take me instead. Take me and kill me . . ."

And Mrs Masters shouted at the Redcaps, "Yeh, go on, you might as well take that silly fat cow instead of him. She'll be about as much use to the army as he bloody well is."

Mrs Masters son is in Burma, and she don't like Mr and Mrs Polson very much. She says her Henry and his mates are fighting the Japs in Burma and all that fat bugger Polson can do is come running back crying to his missis because sweeping up the Naafi canteen in Aldershot is too hard for him.

Mrs Masters says that it would serve that fat bugger Polson right if they sent him out to Burma. We'd win the battles easy then because the Japs would all die laughing at him.

The coppers come then and they rolled Mrs Polson

into the gutter so that the horse wouldn't step on her. And everybody was walking behind the cart, and they was all laughing and clapping and cheering. Mr Polson kept grinning and winking at us, because he knew what was going to happen next.

When it come to the Co-op stables the horse went back inside to eat its dinner and the Redcaps couldn't stop it.

They must be really daft the Redcaps, because everybody knows that the Co-op horse always goes back to the stables to have its dinner at the same time every day. The Co-op horse won't do anything until it's had its dinner.

The Redcaps was all swearing and shouting, and they missed the train because the horse took a long time to eat its dinner. In the end they had to get Billy Jackson's lorry to take Mr Polson back to the army.

My Mam come home from work today, and she looked at the clock and said, "Just look at the time. Harry Polson is due back again."

Chapter Six

Sometimes there's rows and fights in our street. Sometimes two kids start rowing and fighting and then the kids' big brothers and sisters comes out, and then their Mams and Dads and they all starts rowing and fighting.

Johnny Merry is the best fighter in our street, and I'm the next best fighter. Sometimes when us kids are having a fight the men from the pub come to watch us. They makes us fight fair. No kicking, no biting, no scratching or hair pulling. The men says it's only girls who fights like that. They says that men have to stand up square and settle it with their fists.

Sometimes if it's a big kid and a little kid fighting the men stops it.

The men fights with each other as well when they've been in the pub all night, and the women does sometimes. My Mam says I can't play outside the pub, but me and Johnny Merry still does play there. We watches when the men fights. It's ever so good. It's just like on the pictures, when the cowboys fights with each other. But it's no good when the women fights, because they just screeches and pulls each other's hair all the time.

Uncle Sid says that he's the best fighter in the town. He says that he used to be a champion boxer and he can

33

knock anybody out with just one punch. But Uncle Sid says that he won't fight anybody now because he killed a man in the ring once when he was a champion boxer. He says he still feels so guilty about that, he daren't ever hit anybody ever again.

I told my Mam what Uncle Sid had done to that man in the ring, and she laughed and said that the only ring Uncle Sid had ever been in was the Bull Ring in Brummagem. She says that he was a champion all right, but only at running.

But when I told Uncle Sid what my Mam had said, he told me that he'd never told her about him being a champion boxer because he didn't want her to know what he'd done to that man in the ring. Then Uncle Sid showed me some cigarette cards with photos of champion boxers on them, and he showed me the one that was him. The name on the bottom of the card wasn't Uncle Sid's name though, and when I read the name out Uncle Sid said that that was his professional name. He said that all champion boxers had different names to fight under from their real names. The photo didn't look like Uncle Sid either. But he told me that he was a lot younger when the photo was taken, so that was why it didn't look like him now.

When Uncle Sid starts speaking to me again, I'm going to ask him if I can show the photo to Johnny Merry. Because Johnny Merry wants to be a champion boxer when he grows up. I don't want to though. I want to be a paratrooper, like Frankie Savin.

Chapter Seven

It's Waste Paper week at our school. We have to get all our waste paper and take it to school. Then our teacher, her name's Miss Ladwood, gives us our soldier's badges. The badges are only made out of cardboard, because Miss Ladwood says that all the tin has to be used for the war. They're all different sizes. There's big round red badges with Captain on them, and there's small blue round ones with Sergeant on them. And then there's teeny little white square ones with Private on them. There's one badge bigger than all the rest with General written on it. It's a gold one and looks ever so good.

The kid who brings the most waste paper is going to be the General, and the kids who only brings a bit of paper will get the littlest badges, because they'll only be Privates.

We started bringing the paper on Monday morning, and we brings some more every day. Then on Friday the teachers will look at all our different piles and give us our badges. We puts the paper under the big roof in the playground where we plays when its raining. The little kids sleeps there in the warm afternoons. They all lies on stretchers. I used to sleep on the stretchers as well, but not since I've been a big kid.

35

My sweetheart is in our class, her name is Rita Spencer. I like her, but she don't like me, and she won't speak to me. She tells the other girls that she don't like me because I'm too daft and scruffy. Rita Spencer's got long black hair, and she's ever so pretty, and she wears really posh dresses. She lets some of the boys give her piggybacks around the playground when it's playtime. But she won't let me give her a piggyback.

One day she told her friend Sheila Bevin to tell Johnny Merry that she liked him, and that he could give her a piggyback. But Johnny Merry don't like girls, so he wouldn't. But he said that if she liked she could give him a piggyback. He told me that she called him a rude word then. But I don't believe him, because Rita Spencer don't know any rude words, she's too posh.

I'm going to collect lots and lots of paper, so I can be the General. Perhaps Rita Spencer will like me then, and let me give her a piggyback round the playground.

Chapter Eight

We got our badges today. Miss Ladwood was looking at
all the piles of paper under the Big Roof, and Aubrey,
the posh kid, hadn't got a pile at all, because he never
brought any paper with him to school all the week. When
Miss Ladwood was looking at the paper he said to her,
"Please Miss, my Father is bringing my collection when
he comes home for lunch." My Mam says that lunch is
a posh name for dinner.

And Miss Ladwood smiled at him and she patted his
head and said, "That's all right, my dear. Your Father
phoned Miss Brown about it." Miss Brown is our Head
teacher. She's ever so tall.

Aubrey is Miss Ladwood's pet. And Miss Brown's pet
as well. And Rita Spencer likes him now as well, because
she's going to his birthday party next week. None of the
kids in our street have been invited to his party though.
Rita Spencer's swanking because Aubrey sent her a big
card inviting her to the birthday party. She brought it to
school and showed it to everybody. She wouldn't show
it me though. She showed it to Johnny Merry and he run
off with it and then told her that he'd tore it up, and she
started crying and ran to tell on him to Miss Ladwood.

Miss Ladwood went mad! She come running out and

grabbed hold of him, but he got away from her and then she chased him all over the playground. But Miss Ladwood can't run very fast because she's ever so old and bent over, and she's only got one lung and all us kids have got two lungs. I know that because Miss Ladwood showed us a picture of our lungs and told us we'd all got two of them. She said we should go down on our knees every day and thank the Good Lord for blessing us with two healthy lungs. She said that she'd only got one lung because she'd lost the other one and her life was a misery because of that.

I wonder where her other lung went to? Uncle Sid says that if anybody loses anything it just goes to show that they don't deserve to have it in the first place.

I wonder why Miss Ladwood don't deserve to have two lungs?

I didn't manage to collect very much paper. Neither did Johnny Merry. We went to people's houses all round our street, but nearly every time they saw us coming they told us that they hadn't got time to sort out any paper. One man said, "Don't you bloody kids know that there's a bloody war on? I've got enough to bloody do working all the hours God sends to beat the bloody Jerries, let alone sorting out bloody paper for you bloody kids."

Johnny Merry cheeked him, and the man chased us. He couldn't catch Johnny Merry, but he caught me, and he didn't half give me a clout. I run home and told my Mam what the man had done, and she give me another clout for pestering people. It's not fair! Johnny Merry never gets a clout, does he!

Aubrey's Dad come to school in his big car, and Miss Brown and Miss Ladwood and us kids all come out to see him. Aubrey's Dad's car is ever so posh. It's all black and shiny. Nobody else in our street has got a car. Aubrey don't half swank about his Dad's car.

Uncle Sid says that he's got a better car than Aubrey's Dad's car. But it's in a garage and he can't get it out because the road in front of the garage has been blown up by a bomb, and its got a big hole in it.

I told him that I'd help him to fill the hole in, so that he could get his car out, but Uncle Sid said that it wasn't worth the bother because the Jerries would only bomb another hole in the road. So he was going to wait 'til the war finished and get his car out of the garage then.

Aubrey's Dad's car was full to the brim with paper, and Miss Ladwood made me and Johnny Merry get all the paper out of the car and put it under the big roof. It wasn't half hard work. We was both tired out by the time we'd finished.

Then all us kids had to line up, and Miss Brown said, "Children, Captain Jones-Evans has very kindly consented to judge the piles of paper and to present your badges to you. It is an honour to have a distinguished soldier like Captain Jones-Evans to judge our little competition and to give us our badges."

Johnny Merry held his hand up then, and Miss Brown looked ever so sour at him and said all sharp, "Yes, Merry, what is it?"

Johnny Merry said, "Please Miss, Aubrey's Dad's not a real soldier. He's only in the Home Guards. And our Doreen says he only joined them to get out of going into the proper army, because he's scared of being shot at by the Jerries."

Miss Brown went mad then, and tried to clout him, but

39

Johnny Merry dodged and run away. He jumped over the wall and he never come back to school all day.

We all had to stand to attention, and Aubrey's Dad told us that we were little soldiers, and that we had got to do our bit for our King and country like he was doing his bit. And we'd got to be happy and cheerful, and obey Miss Brown and Miss Ladwood at all times. Then he give us our badges.

Aubrey was made the General. And Rita Spencer was made a Captain. All the rest was made Sergeants, except for me and Fatty Polson. We was made Privates.

Then Aubrey's Dad made us all give three cheers for the General, who was Aubrey, and three cheers for the King. I only pretended to cheer, because I was sulking about being only made a Private. I brought as much paper as Letty Dobbs and Tony Perks, and a lot of the other kids, and they was all made Sergeants. Fatty Polson hadn't brought any paper at all. So why did Aubrey's Dad only make me a Private the same as Fatty Polson, I'd like to know?

Chapter Nine

There's a big house called the Hostel at the top end of our street. It's next to Aubrey's house. The Hostel has got lots of bushes and trees all round it, and at the back it's got some big gardens with apples and pears and rassberrys and gusgogs. There's a lot of women living at the Hostel. They all works at the munitions. My Mam always calls them the 'Hostel Girls', and she says that they're all man-mad. I dunno what man-mad means though.

When it's the light nights they all walks arm in arm down the street singing together. Sometimes they calls us kids over and talks to us. Some of them calls me 'Sweetheart' and they gives me a bit of chocolate or a sweet if I run errands for them to the shops. Sometimes they sends me to look round the corner and see if there's a man waiting there. If there is, then I have to run back and tell them what he's doing. And then they sends me back to have another look at him. Sometimes I'm running backwards and forwards for hours and hours.

I don't mind doing that when the man is a Yank, because then I can ask him, "Have you got any gum, Chum?"

Whenever I ask a Yank that he always asks me, "Have you got a sister, Buddy?"

And I say yes, her name's Virgy. Then the Yank says, "Well, I'd like to meet her. I'll take her to a movie, or a dance."

Then I tell him, "Well, you'll have to ask my Mam about that, because I don't think she likes Virgy to go out with the Yanks. My Mam says that she's too young to go out with boys."

"How old is your sister, Buddy?"

"Eleven."

"Jeeze!"

A lot of times when I tell the Yank how old my sister is he don't give me any gum after all.

Of all the Hostel girls Josie is the one I like the best though. She's ever so pretty with goldie-coloured hair, and she comes from Scotland. She kisses me on the cheek and tells me that when I'm grown up she's going to marry me. I like it when she kisses me because she always smells nice.

Hilda, our lodger, kisses me as well sometimes, but she smells funny. A bit like the bike oil Uncle Sid puts on his bike. All the grown-ups who works in the factories smells like that.

My Mam hardly ever kisses me though. Only sometimes when she's been out to the pub with Uncle Sid, and then she hugs me really tight so I can't hardly breathe, and kisses me, and keeps calling me her pitiful fatherless babby. I don't like it when she kisses me though, because she leaves my face all wet and sticky.

There's an old woman named Miss Mason who lives at the Hostel, and Josie says that Miss Mason is in charge, and that all the women have to do what she says. I don't like Miss Mason, because when we goes scrumping in the Hostel gardens she sends her dog out to chase us.

Her dog ripped my trousers one day when me and Johnny Merry was scrumping apples, and we had to climb right up to the top of the tree to get away from it. It kept on barking and trying to jump up after us, and we bombed it with apples, but it wouldn't go away. Then Miss Mason come down the garden with a man who had one of those funny deerstalker hats on and plus-fours, and the man had a walking stick as well, and he was waving it at us and shouting, "I'm going to leather you little blighters. I'm going to teach you a lesson that you won't forget in a hurry!"

He was ever so posh, and Johnny Merry put a posh voice on and shouted back at him, "Oh no you're not, you blighter!"

I was fritted, but it still made me laugh. Johnny Merry does ever such a funny posh voice.

Miss Mason shouted, "You cheeky little blighters! Get down from that tree this instant!"

And Johnny Merry shouted back, "No I won't, you blighter."

Then the man went mad and he started to climb up the tree, and Miss Mason kept saying, "No Rodney, no. Think of your heart. Please Rodney, remember your heart. Come down, Rodney."

But the man wouldn't do what she told him, and then he got stuck halfway up the tree. Some of the Hostel girls come down the garden then and when they saw Rodney up the tree they started laughing and shouting, "Hey ooop, it's bloody Tarzan!"

"And there's bloody Cheetah and his mate as well."

"Let's see you swing, Tarzan!"

And some of the girls kept on going, "Ayiiieeeeeee! Ayiee! Ayiee, Ayiee . . ." just like Tarzan does when he gives his jungle call.

Miss Mason was telling them off, but they still kept on going, "Ayiiieeeeeee Ayiee Ayiee . . ."

After a bit they fetched a long ladder, but Rodney still couldn't climb down because his foot was stuck between two branches. He was roaring and shouting and the Hostel girls was all laughing and Miss Mason was crying and screeching, "Think of your heart, Rodney! Remember your heart!"

Then the fire engine come down the lane at the bottom of the garden, and all the firemen climbed over the fence and they was trampling the bushes and flowers.

Miss Mason stopped crying and told the firemen, "I want those little blighters arrested. I want them to pay for what they've done. Look at all this damage! I want them arrested."

I was really fritted then, because my Mam keeps on telling me that if I get into trouble she'll skin me alive.

Johnny Merry wasn't fritted though. He shouted to the firemen, "I want those blighters arrested, as well."

Then he whispered to me, "I'm going to have a fit when they gets us down. That'll frit 'em."

The firemen told Miss Mason that they couldn't arrest us and she'd have to send for the police to do that. And all the Hostel girls was saying that it was a shame for us, and that we'd only been scrumping a few sour apples, and that we should be let go.

Well, the firemen come up the ladder and they got Rodney down, and then they got me and Johnny Merry down. When we was coming down the ladder Rodney kept on shaking his stick at us and bawling, "I'll teach you a lesson now, you little blighters. I'll teach you not to be rude to me in future. I'll teach you some manners."

But as soon as we was on the ground Johnny Merry did his fit. He does his fit ever so good. It looks just like a real fit. I know what a real fit looks like because Mad Jack has fits on the pavement down town all the time. That's how Johnny Merry learned how to have a fit, because he watches Mad Jack have his.

He holds his breath 'til he turns red and blue, and he shakes all over and makes his eyes go cross-eyed, and he saves up his spit until he's got enough to bubble it out of his mouth. And then he falls on the floor and keeps on bouncing up and down.

When Johnny Merry had his fit all the Hostel girls started screeching, and one of them shouted at Rodney, "Aye ooop, look what you've done to the poor little sod. You've frightened him into a fit, you bullying fat fart!"

Rodney's face went all white, and Miss Mason went all snotty and told the Hostel girl, "Don't you dare blame my fiancé."

The Hostel girl didn't care though. She told Miss Mason, "We all saw what your financy did, didn't we girls?"

And all the girls shouted, "Yeh, we saw it. It's your financy's fault. He's fritted the poor little sod into having a fit."

Rodney put his hand on his chest then, and he said to Miss Mason, "My heart, Grace, my heart."

"Oh you poor lamb," Miss Mason got ever so worried.

"You poor lamb, you must come and lie down immediately." She took him away, and he was groaning and moaning and limping.

The girls was all laughing then, and shouting, "Don't you go rubbing his balls for him, Grace, or you'll finish him off altogether."

"If you has a bit Grace, then you better get on top."

"Don't let him wank for at least a week, Grace. He needs to rest."

As soon as Miss Mason was gone Johnny Merry stopped having his fit. He never keeps having them for too long, because one time when we was down the town we was playing catch with a big stone. And Johnny Merry broke a shop window. When we went to run away a woman caught hold of Johnny Merry and held onto him 'til the shopman come.

Well, Johnny Merry did his fit then, but he had to keep doing it for ever such a long time because the coppers come as well. In the end they took Johnny Merry to the hospital, and he never come out for ages. They made him stay in bed all the time, and they was really strict with him, so he couldn't have any fun at all. So now he only does his fit for a little while, so that he won't have to be took to the hospital again.

When he stopped having his fit, the firemen who was looking after him grinned at each other, and one of them winked and said, "I reckon we've seen a bloody medical miracle here, lads." Then he said to Johnny Merry, "I'll have to get you to show me how to do that, you crafty little sod. It'll come in handy when I wants to work me ticket."

The firemen went away then, and they was all looking

46

backwards at Johnny Merry and shaking their heads and laughing. But all the Hostel girls come crowding around him making a fuss of him, and giving him sweets and bits of chocolate.

They wanted to carry him home, but he wouldn't let them and in the end they let him go. We went down to the railway line and shared the sweets they'd give him. When we was eating the sweets Johnny Merry said, "These are better than them sour apples, aren't they? I reckon I'm going to have another fit in the Hostel garden next week."

Chapter Ten

When it's the dark nights we have to put the blackout curtains up on the windows before we puts the lights on in our house. My Mam says that it's so the Jerry bombers can't see us. She says that before the war all the streets used to be lit up as bright as day by the lamps, and nobody had blackout curtains. There's still a lot of lamp-posts down our street, but they don't light up any more.

It must have been ever so good before the war, because my Mam says that you could buy oranges and bananas from the shops, and anything else you wanted, and there wasn't any rationing. You could buy all the sweets and chocolate that you could eat, and as many toys and books as you could afford.

At school, Miss Ladwood told us that the reason we can't buy any oranges and bananas is because the ships that bring them have all been sunk by the U-boats.

But I think that she's telling fibs, because Aubrey, the posh kid, gets lots of oranges and bananas to eat. And he gets lots of sweets and chocolates as well. And he's got all sorts of toys and books, and a brand new bike.

Uncle Sid says that Mr Jones-Evans gets everything he wants from the Black Market. And he says that if he was running the country then every bugger who buys anything from the Black Market would be put up against the wall and shot.

When he says that my Mam tells him, "Don't be such a hypocrite. You'd be the first bugger to get stuff off the Black Market if you got the chance. And so would everybody else in this country if the truth's known."

When I asked my Mam about it, she told me that rich people can get whatever they want from the Black Market. But they have to pay a lot of money for what they get. And she told me, "If I had the money I'd use the Black Market as well."

I don't know where the Black Market is though. Me and Johnny Merry went down town and we looked all over the place for it. But none of the shops are named Black Market. There's one shop named the Penny Market that sells all sorts of things for a penny or tuppence or thruppence, and there's a butchers' shop named the Meat Market.

I asked the lady in the Penny Market if it was the Black Market. And she roared with laughing and said, "No, my duck, but I wish to Christ it was . . . I'd be in clover then."

Then we went to the Meat Market. There was a big queue of women there, and we had to sneak to the front of the queue. The butcher man was chopping some bones with a big chopper, and his face was all red and sweaty, and when we asked him if this was the Black Market, some of the women cheered. And the man stared at us, and his eyes went all bulgy and his face went all purple, and he crashed the chopper down onto the block, and he picked up a great big bone and chucked it at us. It only missed us because we both ducked ever so quick. Then he picked up another great big bone and chucked that at us as well, and we run out of the shop, and the bone crashed into the doorway over our heads.

I dunno why the butcher man chucked bones at us, because we was only looking for the Black Market. I was going to tell my Mam about the butcher man chucking bones at us, but then I remembered that she'd only give me a tanning for pestering people, so I didn't tell her.

Isn't it funny how many things are called Black . . . like the Black Market, and Black Pudding and the Black Out.

When we have the Black Out the Air Raid Warden has to come round and see that there's no lights shining from the houses. Mrs Masters don't do a good Black Out though. She always has lights shining through her windows because her Black Out curtains are all holey. She said that the moths ate the curtains. She told me one day that the moths were Adolf Hitler's secret weapon and that he'd sent them all over to England when the war broke out so they could eat all the blackout curtains and let the lights shine out so that the Jerry bombers could see where we was hiding.

Our Air Raid Warden is Mr Bent. He's got a shop down in Orchid Street. That's down to the bottom of our street then turn left down West Street and then turn right and that's Orchid Street. Mr Bent walks ever so tall and straight and swings his arms just like he's marching. My Mam says that's because he was a Sergeant-Major in the Guards before he got too old for the army. That's the proper Guards, not the Home Guards. He puts wax on his moustache and makes it look as if he's got two needles sticking out from under his nose. My Mam says that he thinks he's still in the army, the way he carries on. Because when he comes round at nights to see if the Black Out curtains are up, he stands in the street and shouts, "Number 44, put that bedroom light out! Number 37, there's an inch of light showing at the left-hand side of your window. Number 18, get that curtain mended. There is a tear in it approximately two inches right centre!"

Then he shouts, "I shall return to this position at 2030 hours. If the faults are not rectified, you will all be placed on a charge."

When he comes to Mrs Masters' house he shouts, "Number 33, your curtains are made of holes tied together with string. Get them changed immediately."

Mrs Masters always shouts back, "Piss off Number 15 and get your own curtains fixed. Your windows looks like the bloody Blackpool illuminations."

Number 15 is the number of Mr Bent's shop down Orchid Street, you see.

I wonder why Mrs Masters talks about Blackpool so much? Perhaps she's been there for a holiday?

Chapter Eleven

The Jerries dropped bombs on us last night and I wasn't fritted. But Uncle Harold's still in bed with his nervous breakdown. We was having a cup of cocoa and a piece of bread and jam for our supper, because my Mam said that we'd all got to go to bed early because Uncle Sid was tired out. He didn't look tired out to me, because he kept on jumping out of his chair to go into the back kitchen where my Mam was and having a play wrestle with her, and she kept on telling him, "Later Sid! Let's get the kids to bed first."

Then the sirens went off all over the place and Uncle Sid didn't half swear. "Bloody soddin' Jerries!" he said. "First time for bloody soddin' months I've been on a promise, and the bloody soddin' Jerries has to come over and spoil it!"

I was glad the Jerries had come over though, because I didn't want to go to bed early. I wasn't a bit tired, even if Uncle Sid was. It's not fair, is it? When I'm tired my Mam don't put Uncle Sid to bed early, does she! So why should I have to go to bed early just because he's tired?

While the sirens was going we could hear Mr Bent shouting outside, "Number 33, get those lights out! There is an air raid in progress."

And we heard Mrs Masters shout at him, "I know there's a bloody air raid in progress, you silly old bugger. Does you think I'm deaf?"

"I shan't tell you again, Number 33. Get those lights out now or you're on a charge."

"Oh, piss off!"

The next minute Mrs Masters come into our house, and she asked me Mam if she could stay with us while the Jerries was here. Then Miss Freeman come as well. So we all got into the pantry under the stairs. My Mam, Uncle Sid, Hilda, Granny Smith, Uncle Harold, our Virgy and me, Mrs Masters and Miss Freeman. And we had a bottle of pop and some lighted candles. I had my piece of jam as well because I hadn't had time to eat it.

We could hear the Jerry bombers coming nearer. They was going *errrummm, errrummm, errummm, errummm* and getting ever so loud, and Mrs Masters looked fritted and said, "The buggers are coming for us this time, you know. They're right overhead. They're after the munitions factory I reckon."

"God, I hope not!" My Mam looked a bit fritted as well. "Think of all those poor young wenches working there tonight."

Then Granny Smith had one of her funny turns, and she shouted, "I'm going to give them noisy sods a smack in the chops."

And before anybody could stop her she grabbed one of the candles and run out into the back garden. And we could hear her shouting at the Jerries.

Uncle Harold had his nervous breakdown again then. He laid down on the floor with his hands over his head shouting, "Will somebody please shoot that silly old cow! Will somebody please shoot that silly old cow! Will somebody please shoot that silly old cow!"

Miss Freeman started to pray, and Uncle Sid got all shirty and said, "Close the bloody door, somebody. There's a terrible cold draft in here. I wish your bloody Mam would close the bloody doors after her, Effie. She's got no consideration for anybody else, has she."

The Jerries weren't half noisy then. They sounded like they was only upstairs, *ERRUMMMM ERRUMMM, ERRUMMM, ERRUMMM*. And My Mam got up and said, "I'm going to fetch my Mam in."

Hilda said, "I'll come with you, Effie."

And then the bombs went off!

There was ever such a lot of loud bangs and everything shook and rattled, and the plaster fell down onto Uncle Sid's head, and because he puts a lot of Brylcream on his hair all the white bits stuck to it and he looked as if he'd been out in the snow.

Our Virgy screamed and Miss Freeman started singing. 'Nearer my God to Thee', until Uncle Sid shouted at her, "Shurrup you silly old mare, we've come a sight too bloody close to Him already!"

"What about my Mam? Where's my Mam?" my Mam shouted, and she run out of the pantry, and we all came out as well. Except for Uncle Harold, because he was still laying on the floor having his nervous breakdown.

My Mam run out of the back door, and just as she went Granny Smith come in through the front door and started switching all the downstairs lights on. She was all excited, and she kept saying, "There, I've see them cheeky buggers off! They won't come waking me up again in a hurry! They soon run away when I went out to them, didn't they. Good riddance to bad rubbish! Let them stay up their own end of the street and play their own bloody families up! I'll give them a bloody good smack in the chops if they ever comes near me again!"

"Number 31, put those lights out. Or you'll be on a charge!" Mr Bent come shouting outside our house.

And then the sirens went for the All Clear and Mrs Masters told him, "Piss off, you silly old sod, and find something useful to do."

Everybody run out into the street then to see where the bombs had gone off.

"Look down there," Uncle Sid told us, and we could see flames and smoke and hear the fire engines coming clanging their bells.

"It's Orchid Street that's got it, I reckon," Hilda said, and then farther over the other way we could see some more flames.

"That's Morton Road or one of them streets down there," Uncle Sid reckoned.

My Mam come running up to us then and she got hold of Granny Smith and shook her really hard. "Don't you ever frighten me like that again, Mam," she was shouting at her at the top of her voice. "Don't you ever run out like that again."

Then Mr Griffin, who lives round the top corner, come up to us and said to Uncle Sid, "Come on, we'll go down and see if we can help those poor buggers."

And him and Uncle Sid went running off down the road towards Orchid Street. And after a bit a lot of the other grown-ups went running down there as well. But they made all us kids stay up in our own street, and a couple of the grown-ups stayed with us and made us all keep together.

Some of the kids was crying, but I wasn't because it was exciting. Just like the pictures really.

Then the grown-ups came back and they made all us kids go to bed. My Mam said that nobody was killed down Orchid Street, and only two houses had been blown up. She said that all the people from Orchid Street was in the big air raid shelter when the bombs went off and that was why nobody was killed.

Nobody from our street ever goes into the big shelter, because they don't like the people down Orchid Street. We was going to have a shelter for our street once, but they made it into an ARP post instead. My Mam says that she wouldn't ever go into an air raid shelter anyway because it's better to stay in your own house under the stairs. You can choose your own company then and you don't have to put up with the drunks and the scruffs.

I wonder if my Mam means the drunks and scruffs that Mrs Jones-Evans was talking about the other day. She was in a shop down town where me and Johnny Merry was and I heard her telling another woman, who was wearing a fur coat, that living in our street was a misery because she was surrounded by drunks and scruffs. I wonder who she means?

Chapter Twelve

Me and Johnny Merry went down to the bombed buildings today. We went to Orchid Street first, and then we
went down Morton Road. Johnny Merry says that he was
standing in the middle of Morton Road last night when
the bombs went off. He says it was ever so good, just
like the pictures. But at first I didn't believe him, because
whenever the Jerry bombers comes over everybody has
to hide, so he couldn't have been standing in the middle
of the road. But he explained how he'd escaped from
his house while Doreen and her boyfriend was having a
Doo in the front room, and he'd crept out the back way
and he'd gone down Morton Road. He says that he heard
the bombs come whistling down, and he threw himself
over a wall, like the soldiers do on the pictures, and the
bombs missed him. Then he got up and run to see if he
could save anybody from the bombed buildings. He said
that there was dead people all over the place. One man
was sitting on the lav with no clothes on, and he hadn't
got a head. It had been blown off his shoulders. Then
when Johnny Merry went to look, he saw the man's head
grinning up at him from down the lav. He said that he
thought the head was still alive, because the eyes kept
on winking at him.

Johnny Merry said that when the fire engines come he helped the firemen to put the fires out, and to rescue a lot of people who was covered by bricks. Just as they'd finished rescuing all the people a parachute come down with a Jerry hanging on it. Johnny Merry said that the Jerry was dressed like a nun and he had a tommy-gun. All the firemen was scared to go near the Jerry, but Johnny Merry run after him and chased him for miles, and then jumped on him and knocked him out and captured him. The coppers and the Home Guards come then and took the Jerry to a prison camp.

Johnny Merry said that the coppers and the Home Guards and the firemen told him that he was the bravest boy that they'd ever seen, and that they was going to give him a medal for what he'd done. He's going to be took to London next week and the King is going to give him the medal then.

I wish I could capture a Jerry and get a medal. I bet Rita Spencer would like me then.

There was a lot of men and women clearing the rubbish up in Orchid Street. There was glass all over the road, and none of the houses had any windows left.

There was a copper there as well, and when he saw us he told us to clear off. He said that he'd got orders to shoot looters and desperados. But he was grinning when he said that, so I don't know if he was telling fibs or not.

So then we went down Morton Road, so that Johnny

60

Merry could show me the lav with the man's head inside it.

There was a whole row of houses that had been bombed down there, and there was glass and bricks and all sorts of stuff laying all over the place. I could smell gas in the air, and there was a lot of coppers there and ropes tied all across the street, and there was a a lot of people and kids standing behind the ropes, and some of the women and kids was crying.

When me and Johnny Merry went to creep under the ropes and go nearer the bombed houses a copper shouted at us, and a woman took hold of us and told us, "No, my ducks, don't you go any nearer. There's a gas main broke to pieces and there could be an explosion from it."

Some of the houses had fallen into big piles, and I heard a man behind me say that they couldn't start shifting the rubble to find the bodies until the gasmen had mended the mains, because even a spark could could cause a blow-up.

There was a woman next to us who was all white faced and staring, and when I asked her if there was really some dead people in the bombed houses she started to cry, and the man put his arm round her and told her, "There there, my duck, keep your chin up. There's a good chance that they'll find your folks alive once they can start shifting the rubble."

But the woman just kept on crying and crying.

After a bit I didn't want to stay there any more, because everybody was so sad looking, and so many people was crying. It was making me feel all funny and like crying as well, and I didn't know what to do to stop feeling

61

funny like that. So in the end I just went off by myself and left Johnny Merry there.

I went up into the town then and wandered about a bit. But I still felt all funny and sorrowful-like. So I went back home and sat by myself in the lav for ever such a long time.

Then Fatty Polson come to call for me, and we went to see if we could scrump some gusgogs from the Hostel gardens. I like the gusgogs when they're all green and sharp tasting. When they're sort of reddy purple they're too soggy and sicky. We got our pockets all full before Miss Mason's dog could get us, and we went down to the railway tunnel to eat them. I ate that many that I had a bellyache.

Fatty Polson said, "Lets play at summat."

But I didn't really want to play at anything. I kept on remembering how all the people was crying down in Morton Road, and I kept on feeling all funny and sorrowful-like. And I kept thinking about that man who's head was down the lav and I thought. "What if it had been my Mam's head down the lav?"

Then Fatty Polson said, "What's you crying for, Specs?" And I got up and run away from him, and went and hid in the bushes on the railway bank.

I cried for ever such a long time before I felt better. Then I felt really hungry, so I went back home to have my dinner, and my Mam shouted at me, "Where have you been, you little sod? I've been shouting at you for for ages to come for your dinner."

And Granny Smith told her, "You ought to give the little bugger a good tanning. He's a wicked little bugger, so he is."

But I didn't care about my Mam shouting at me. I was just glad that our house hadn't been bombed, and that her head wasn't down the lav.

But I wouldn't have minded if Granny Smith's head had been down the lav though. Miserable old cow!

Chapter Thirteen

Hitler has only got one ball
Goering has two but very small,
Himmler has something simmler,
And poor old Goebbels
Has no balls
At all!

I learned that song today. It's ever so good, ain't it? Me and Johnny Merry were marching like soldiers and singing it, and Old Mrs Berrod from West Street was cleaning her front doorstep when we went past her, and she told us off.

"You foul-mouthed little sods!" That's what she called us, "I'm going up to tell your parents about you."

Old Mrs Berrod always wears a big black hat and a pinafore. Even when she's going to the shops down town. She don't like me and Johnny Merry, because whenever Johnny Merry sees her he always shouts, "If you can't fight, wear a big black hat!"

I don't think she likes any of the kids really, because she's always going to the parents and telling on them for different things. My Mam says that if Mrs Berrod lived in India she'd be sacred. I dunno what she means when she says that, but Hilda always laughs.

Hilda's always laughing at what my Mam tells her. Tonight when we was having our supper my Mam told Hilda that Uncle Sid is useless, because he only has to have a sniff of it and he comes his duff. He's a five-second Superman. That's what she said.

Hilda didn't half laugh.

I asked my Mam what she mean't and she told me not to be so nosey. She said that there'll be plenty of time to poke my nose into things when I'm grown up.

Then Hilda said, "Well I hope he'll be able to poke it farther up than Harold can."

And they both started laughing again.

When old Mrs Berrod told us off we kept on marching up and down outside her gate singing our song to try to get her to chase us. But all she did was chuck her bucket of water at us, and it went all over my legs and soaked my boots and socks.

We pretended to run away then, but when we got round the corner we crept back. Old Mrs Berrod's entry runs downhill, and we likes to roll big stones down it because they makes a noise and then she comes out after us.

That's what we did as soon as she went back inside her house. We rolled some really big stones down the entry, and then we waited for her to come out and chase us. But she didn't come out, so we rolled a lot more stones down.

And then a whole lot of water come down onto us and soaked us both.

"That caught you napping, didn't it, you little sods!" old Mrs Berrod shouted, and I looked up and saw her leaning out of a window right at the top of the house. She was waving a pisspot at us and grinning like a Cheshire Cat.

"Just stay there a minute," she told us. "There's plenty more where this come from. I've still got my old man's pot full."

When we was running away, Johnny Merry said, "Phewwww! It don't half stink."

Fatty Polson and some of the other kids was playing on the corner and when we come up to them, they all started holding their noses.

"Phewwww!"

"What a stink!"

"Go away, you stinks!"

Then they all started dancing around us and singing, "Who's a little stinky drawers . . . Who's a little stinky drawers . . . Who's a little stinky drawers?"

And they run away laughing when we was going to get them.

"What shall we do?" I asked Johnny Merry, because I was fritted of going home all smelly. "My Mam won't half give me a tanning for spoiling me clothes."

Johnny Merry didn't care though. Because he knew that he wouldn't get a tanning when he went home. It arn't fair. He never gets a tanning, does he.

"I'm going home," he told me. "I'm going to put me other clothes on. Your Mam's at work now," he said. "You can go home and put your other clothes on before she comes back."

"But Uncle Harold's there, and he'll tell her when she comes back. Can't I come to your house with you?"

"No. Our Doreen don't like you, because she had that

row with your Mam. See you tomorrow." And then he run off and left me.

All the wet was still dripping down me, and it smelled ever so bad, and I nearly started to cry because I knew that I was never going to go home ever again. I'd have to run away, because my Mam would kill me if she found out why I was stinking like this. She told me after the last time old Mrs Berrod had been to my house to carry on about me and Johnny Merry, that if I ever played old Mrs Berrod up again, then she'd kill me, as sure as God made little apples, she'd kill me.

I thought, 'I'll have to run away'. But I didn't know where to run away to. And then I remembered that every boy who run away, run away to sea. It didn't half cheer me up when I remembered that. Because in all the stories all the boys who run away to sea come back as big men with lots of gold and treasure. I thought about joining the pirates and fighting with cutlasses and pistols like they did. I saw a picture once about the pirates and it was ever so good. And ever since then I always wanted to be a pirate. So I started to run away.

I thought, 'If I run fast I'll be able to get to sea and be a pirate before its gets dark.'

I run up past the Hostel and Josie was coming down the road, and she saw me.

"Where are you going, Specs?"

"I'm running away to sea, Josie."

When she got close to me she went, "Phewww, what's that smell?"

"It's me. That's why I'm running away to sea. Because my Mam will kill me if I goes home all stinky like this."

Josie laughed then. "Tell you what, Specs, you can run

away to sea next week. You come back with me now, and I'll get you cleaned up. Then you can go home to your Mam."

At first I shook my head. Because I really want to be a pirate. But then Josie told me, "I've got some chocolate in my room. Do you want a bit of it?"

So I went back with her. And she cleaned me all up. Then she give me a piece of chocolate and kissed me on the cheek, and sent me home.

I'm going to marry Josie when I grow up, and we can run away to sea with each other then and both be pirates.

Chapter Fourteen

'Jacky Five Stones' is the craze this week. All the kids are playing it. It's ever such a good game. You have to start with one stone and see how many you can end up catching. The kid who catches the most is the winner and keeps the 'Jackies'.

There's a shop down town that sells 'Jackies'. They're painted all different colours and they're all the same size and weight. I should like to buy some, but I never have enough money. Aubrey Jones-Evans and his posh pals buys lots of Jackies but the rest of us have to use stones and pebbles. Aubrey Jones-Evans and his posh pals looks down their noses at our Jackies and laughs at them, and they won't play 'Jacky Five Stones' with us because we haven't got proper Jackies. I'd really like to be able to buy some proper Jackies, then I could play with Aubrey and his pals and win all their Jackies off them. That would make them laugh on the other side of their faces.

When you can't buy proper Jackies you have to find stones that are the right sort of shape and size to be Jackies. They have to be a bit squarish, and all the same size, not too big, but just right. The best place to find the stones is down the Council Yard where the road-menders keeps all the gravel and stones for the roads. The road-menders have got a horse and cart down the Council Yard as well. The horse is ever so old, and walks really really slow.

My Mam says that the horse is like the Council blokes who mends the roads, they're all ready for the Knackers Yard as well. She says that when the Council blokes do any work they've only got two speeds, Dead Slow and Stop! She keeps on telling Uncle Harold that he ought to go and get a job on the Council.

"It would suit you down to the ground, our Harold. Because those council blokes likes work just about as much as you do."

Uncle Harold gets all shirty when she tells him that. "You know very well, our Effie, that Council employment is beneath me. I've got a poetic soul. God put me on this earth to observe the follies of my fellow man, and to record my observations in a great work of art. I may write it as a poem, a play, or a novel, I haven't decided yet."

"Well you couldn't ask for a better job then, Shakespeare," my Mam tells him. "Because that's all the bloody Council blokes does all day is to lean on their shovels and observe the follies of their fellow man. And you'll be able to do all the writing you want when you're having your tea breaks, because you'll be sitting down for hours on end then."

Whenever my Mam has a go at Uncle Harold, Hilda always takes his part and sticks up for him, "My Harold is too sensitive to work with all those rough men. And, anyway, he's not strong enough to use a pick and shovel. Just look at how thin he is."

"You're right there, Hilda my duck, I've seen more meat on a bicycle chain," my Mam tells her. "When

72

you has a bit, it must feel like you're wrapping your legs around Famine."

"Maybe so, Effie. But you know what they say, 'The nearer the bone, the sweeter the meat'," Hilda says, and they both start laughing then.

Me and Letty Dobbs went down to the Council Yard after school today to look for 'Jackies'. I like Letty. If she wasn't a girl I'd be best friends with her. But you can't be best friends with a girl, can you? Only pansies are best friends with girls. But I always let Letty play with us when she wants to. She's good at a lot of things. She can climb the trees nearly as good as Johnny Merry and climb the roofs nearly as good as me.

She's a good runner as well. She tucks her skirt into her knickers and races all the boys. Johnny Merry is the only one who can beat her.

And she's good at can-walking. Her Mam makes her cans for her. She gets dried milk tins and makes the holes ever so smooth for the strings to go through. And then she measures the strings so that they're just right for Letty to grab hold of and keep the cans pulled up tight against her feet.

When I make cans I can never get the holes smooth and the tin cuts through the string after a bit.

Letty's a good fighter as well. She made Fatty Polson's nose bleed yesterday, and he run home to tell his Mam. Mrs Polson come waddling up the road, gasping ever so loud, and told Letty Dobbs that she was nothing but a bloody rotten tomboy, and she ought to behave like a girl should behave instead of like a bloody hooligan. Mrs

Polson said that Letty ought to be bloody well ashamed of herself for bullying a poor defenceless boy like Fatty whose father is away at the war fighting for his King and country.

Letty didn't care though, because Fatty Polson is bigger than her, and he started the fight in the first place. Letty's Dad is at the war. He's a Commando, and Letty says that she's going to be a Commando when she's big enough.

While me and Letty was looking for Jackies in the Council Yard the dustcart come in. We hid behind the stone pile because the dustcart driver don't like kids and he always chases us out of the yard when he sees us. His name is 'Death at the Feast'. That's what everybody calls him because he always looks so miserable. My Mam says that he should have been an undertaker. She says that with his sour face he's wasted driving the dustcart, he should be driving the hearse instead.

He's got some Ities working on the dustcart with him. They're prisoners of war, but they work on the dustcart because the grown-ups says that they're harmless. Whenever the man on the wireless talks about the Ities fighting, Uncle Sid shouts out, "Fighting? Fighting? The bloody Ities don't even know what the word means. They've only got reverse gears on their tanks."

My Mam give Uncle Sid one of her looks and told him, "That's the sort of tank that would suit you then. You'd have done well if you'd joined the Itie army. They'd have made you a general by now."

Uncle Sid looked ever so fierce, and he pointed to his head. "You can't see the memories that I've got in here. The desert sun has blazed down on me, I'll have you know."

74

"Oh really!" My Mam got all snotty then, "Is that what melted your brains?"

My Mam likes one of the Ities that works on the dustcart, because she says he looks just like Errol Flynn and when he comes up our street to empty the dustbins she always waves and smiles at him. She always asks him, "Hello, Errol Flynn, how are you today, you gorgeous beast?"

He grins at her then and bows and kisses his hands to her and keeps on saying, "Bella, Bella, Bella!"

Then 'Death at the Feast' shouts at him, "Get them bloody dustbins emptied, Mussolini, and let's have less of the bloody 'Bella, Bella'."

Then 'Death at the Feast' tells my Mam, "Don't waste your breath speaking to that ignorant bugger, Missus, he don't spake a word of English, and anyway you didn't ought to be intercorsing with the enemy."

"He might understand more English than you thinks," my Mam tells him. "And I'll intercorse with whoever I wants to intercorse with, so just mind your own business."

Doreen Merry was walking past one day when my Mam said that to 'Death at the Feast', and she laughed ever so nasty and said ever so loud to 'Errol Flynn', "You want's to watch her, Mate. She's only after you because she can't get a Yank."

And 'Errol Flynn' bowed to Doreen, and kissed his hands to her and said, "Bella, Bella, Bella!"

I thought that my Mam would go mad at Doreen then. But she didn't. She only smiled all sarcastic and said ever so sweet, "A little bird tells me that there's another Yank on the way to this street, Doreen. Only he ain't being sent over from Yankee-land."

Doreen went all red in the face and walked away ever so quick. Anyway, me and Letty Dobbs was hiding behind the stone heap and watching 'Death at the Feast' and the Ities.

'Death at the Feast' made the Ities get right into the back of the dustcart and sort through all the rubbish. The Ities was getting ever so dirty and dusty, and they was all talking in their own language, and it sounded as if they was cussing and swearing. They chucked out all sorts of things, bits of wire, bottles, jam-jars, rags, rabbit-skins, old clothes, and 'Death at the Feast' looked at everything, put what he wanted into an old sack on the ground behind him, and chucked the stuff he didn't want back into the cart.

"What's he going to do with all that stuff?" Letty whispered. Letty's a bit slow sometimes, you know. Girls don't seem to know what boys knows. So I told her.

"He's going to sell it."

"Phooo, who'd be daft enough to buy rubbish that's been chucked away!" she said, ever so scornful. I told you that she was a bit slow sometimes, didn't I!

"The Rag and Bone man will buy it. Filthy Charlie."

She still didn't really believe me, so I just said, "Shurrup and listen."

The Ities had got out of the dustcart and they was all jabbering to each other, and they looked as they was getting shirty.

Then one of them, who had grey hair, pointed at the sack of stuff that 'Death at the Feast' had collected, and said, "Every day you take this and get money from old Filthee Charlee, and give nothing to we. That not good."

He sounded just like Tonto does when he talks to the Lone Ranger, so that's what I'm going to name him.

76

'Death at the Feast' looked really sour. "Who does you think that you're talking to, Mussolini?"

"I talk you," Tonto told him. "Every day you promise to give we one cigarette for every man, but you never give us nothing."

"I don't sell this stuff," 'Death at the Feast' said, "I gives it to the Government to help in the War Effort."

What a big liar! I've seen him sell stuff to Filthy Charlie at the Rag and Bone Yard lots of times. I was going to shout to Tonto to tell 'Death at the Feast' that he spoke with forked tongue. But then I thought that I'd better not, because we'd only get chased off if I did.

"You no tell truth!" Tonto was shaking his head. "You take this every day. Get money for it. But you never give we cigarette that you promise. We get very dirty finding things for you in rubbish."

Oh, I forgot to tell you before, but the Ities lives in a camp in the fields, and a lorry brings them to work and takes them back to the camp every day. And there's a corporal comes with the lorry and the Ities has to do what he says. The corporal's an old man with grey hair and his face is ever so brown and wrinkled and he's got a lot of medal ribbons. Every time he tells anybody anything he always says, "When I was out in India . . ." so everybody calls him 'Gunga Din'.

'Death at the Feast' was getting shirty now, I could tell. "If you don't shurrup and mind your own business, Mussolini, I'll report you to the Camp Commandant and you'll be put on a bloody fizzer. You won't come out of that camp again until the bloody war's over. Now just sod off."

The army lorry come back into the yard then, and

77

'Gunga Din' got out and all the Ities run to him, and Tonto was telling him what 'Death at the Feast' had done.

'Gunga Din' come over to 'Death at the Feast' and called him a miserable tight robbing bastard. And 'Death at the Feast' called him a bloody Itie lover, and said that he was going to report 'Gunga Din' to the Camp Commandant as well.

"I'll get you sent to the bloody desert, and you can take them soddin' Ities back there with you when you goes," 'Death at the Feast' was bawling and shouting.

Then 'Gunga Din' said, "When I was out in India this is what I used to do to miserable tight robbing bastards like you." And he hit 'Death at the Feast' and sent him flying, and all the Ities cheered. Only they wasn't cheering like we cheers. They was shouting something like, "*Viva Viva! Bene Bene!*"

That's a daft way to cheer, ain't it!

"Does you want another?" 'Gunga Din' asked 'Death at the Feast'. But he only shouted, "I'm going to tell the police on you!" And he got up and went running out of the yard.

Tonto looked ever so worried then, and he asked 'Gunga Din', "That man he make trouble for you, yes? I very sorry this happen."

'Gunga Din' laughed and shook his head. "When I was out in India I knew the bloke what's the Superintendent of Police here. He's an old mate of mine. And the Commandant likes me too much to have me sent away from him. When I was out in India I was his batman for years." Then they all got onto the army lorry and went off.

"Come on quick," I told Letty, and we run and picked

up the old sack with all the stuff in it and we carried it between us to the Rag and Bone yard and sold it all to Old Charlie.

We bought ever such a lot of proper 'Jackies' with the money we got and divided them between us. Tomorrow I'm going to play 'Jacky Five Stones' with Aubrey and his posh pals, and win all their 'Jackies' off them.

It's been a really good day today.

Chapter Fifteen

We've got a rabbit farm at our house. That's what Uncle Sid calls it. We got it last week. We're going to grow all our own rabbits to eat. I'm fed-up with it already though, because Uncle Sid sends me out collecting dandelions all day, and its the holidays and all the rest of the kids are playing while I'm looking for dandelions.

It was easy to find them at first, but now I've stripped the lane and the rubbish tip, and I have to go all over the place to find them.

There was a lot down the allotments but the men chases me off when I go down there, because they reckon I'm pinching stuff from their allotments. One man found some lettuces in my sack and he clouted me, and told me if he caught me down by his patch again he'd tell the coppers on me. It wasn't fair because I hadn't pinched them from his patch. I pinched them from the patch next to his. Anyway, it's only like scrumping arn't it? And nobody fetches the coppers when they catches the kids scrumping. They just clouts us.

Uncle Sid bought the rabbits and a big hutch and a little hutch from a bloke that he works with. There's a lady rabbit and a man rabbit, and some babby rabbits. We call the lady a doe, and the man a buck, but we just calls the little ones the babbies. We keep the buck in the small hutch away from the others, because Uncle Sid says that he'll eat the babbies if he's left alone with them.

My Mam says that if that's true, then how come there's so many bloody rabbits running around the fields? If they all eats each other, there wouldn't be any of them left by now, would there?

Uncle Sid shakes his head and grins when she says that, and my Mam goes mad then and shouts at him, "Don't you smirk at me, Know-All, because you knows nothing! You big headed bugger!"

Uncle Sid reckons that we shall soon have enough rabbits to eat ourselves and sell them to all the neighbours as well. He says that he'll cut out the Gyppo who brings rabbits around to sell, because the Gyppo's rabbits are wild ones and they're all tough and scrawny. Uncle Sid says that our rabbits will be soft and tender because they don't have to do any work, and they feeds on the fat of the land. Uncle Sid says that he's made a scientific study of what rabbits eat, and he's feeding ours on a special scientific diet which will make them gigantic. He says that when the neighbours sees our rabbits they'll be clamouring to buy them. He says that we'll make a fortune.

My Mam says, "How the bloody hell can you call dandelions a scientific diet? Every rabbit in the country eats dandelions."

Then Uncle Sid looks all wise and tells her, "That just goes to show how much you knows about rabbits, Effie. The wild 'uns are too stupid to eat the proper sort of dandelions that will make them gigantic. That's why they're so small and weedy."

"Oh, I see," My Mam says. "And does Specs know which are the proper sort of dandelions? Because the ones he brings home look just like ordinary dandelions to me."

Uncle Sid started speaking to me again when he bought the rabbits. He's being ever so nice to me, and he bought me a comic yesterday. It was *The Beano*, but I'd sooner have had *Wizard* or *The Rover*, because I can read ever so good, and there's some good stories in *The Rover* and *The Beano*. There's 'Red Circle', all about a public school, and there's 'Wilson the Wonder Man', and 'Alf, the Tough of the Track'.

When I moan about having to collect dandelions all day, Uncle Sid promises that he'll cut me in on the profits when we go into full production. He says that then I'll be the richest kid in the street. He says that the Jones-Evanses will be paupers compared to us. And he's promised my Mam a fur coat as well, but my Mam didn't seem very excited when he promised that. She only sniffed, and said that if she wanted a bloody rabbit-fur coat she could get one from Filthy Charlie's yard, thank you very much!

Uncle Harold likes the rabbits. He takes a chair down the back garden and sits outside the hutches all day watching them. He says that he's communing with nature.

Hilda said to my Mam, "I hope that watching those rabbits going at it will remind him what his own bloody donger's for. Because it's been so long since we had a bit that I'm starting to forget what it feels like."

My Mam laughed and told her, "Sid's donger's never in long enough for me to be able to remember what it feels like. 'Brief Encounter' arn't the word for it."

I saw that film *Brief Encounter*. It was about a railway station, and a woman kept getting smoke in her eye, and a man kept getting the smoke back out of her eye. It was a rotten film!

Chapter Sixteen

I went down the back garden with some dandelions today and Uncle Harold was sitting on the chair bending forwards with his head stuck right inside the big rabbit hutch.

"What's you sitting like that for, Uncle Harold?" I asked him.

"I'm just seeing what it feels like to be in the Condemned Cell waiting to be executed," he told me.

"Well it must stink a bit," I told him ever so quick. "Because you's got your nose in the rabbit poo'." Ha ha ha ha ha! That was a good one, wasn't it!

But Uncle Harold didn't laugh, he just stayed sitting with his head inside the hutch, and the rabbits was all staring at him as if they didn't know what he was doing in there.

"I'm greatly troubled, Specs." Uncle Harold was all sorrowful-like. "I am questioning the moral right of what Sidney Tompkin is doing with these little bunnies."

"Well, Uncle Sid ain't really doing anything with them, is he, Uncle Harold! It's me who has to clean their hutches out, and collect all the dandelions for them to eat, and fetch their straw from the Co-op stables. Anyway, what do you mean, Uncle Harold, when you say moral rights?"

"I mean, Specs, that these dear litle bunnies should be free to run and play, and enjoy themselves like all of God's creatures. They have the right to life, liberty and the pursuit of happiness. Instead of which they are imprisoned here against their will, awaiting death. Oh it's terrible, Specs! It's terrible! The only thing that these poor little bunnies have got to look forward to is the stewpot! Their funeral wreath will be a Spanish onion and a sprig of parsley!"

He started crying then, and buried his face in the straw.

"The rabbits wants their dinner, Uncle Harold," I told him. "You'll have to take your head out so I can put the dandelions in."

"Harold? Harold? Come here this instant!" Granny Smith started screeching for him from the house then. "Harold, I wants me back scratched."

Urrggghhh! That's summat that I hates doing. Scratching Granny Smith's back for her. She sits on a chair, and makes us stand behind her and push our hands down inside the back of her frock and scratch the pimples on her back because they itches her. She makes us do it for hours and hours and it feels horrible. All sweaty and scabby under your nails.

I always hides, and our Virgy does too when Granny Smith wants her back scratched, so she always cops hold of Uncle Harold now and makes him do it. She says he does it the nicest anyway, because me and Virgy digs our nails in too much and hurts her.

When he pulled his head out of the hutch he had rabbit poo stuck all over his face, and I told him, "You've got rabbit poo on your face, Uncle Harold."

86

He just smiled all sorrowful-like, and he shook his head. "No, Specs, don't call it poo. Call it instead the symbol of man's inhumanity. Specifically, Sidney Tompkin's inhumanity to bunnies."

Then he told the rabbits, "Farewell, dear little friends. I shall return. Take comfort in knowing that though all the world betray thee, one sword at least thy rights shall guard, one faithful harp shall praise thee."

Then he went off up the garden calling, "I'm coming, Mother. I'm coming. Prepare your pimples, for I am coming."

He's really weird sometimes, my Uncle Harold is.

Chapter Seventeen

Some of the kids from our street goes to the Sunday School at the Chapel. Our Virgy loves going to Sunday School. She goes in the morning and the afternoon, and then she goes to the Band of Hope on Wednesdays, and the Junior Bible Class on Fridays. She always gets the prize for the best attendance at Sunday School. At first my Mam used to like Virgy going to Sunday School, but now she's doesn't, because she says that just lately Virgy's got religion on the brain.

Virgy's started saying that we're all sinners in our house, and that we should be Seeking redemption at the Mercy Seat. She says that she's been Washed in the Blood of the Lamb, and that when the Day of Judgement dawns she'll be the only one in our house who will be taken into Paradise to sit at the right hand of the Master. She says that the rest of us will be Cast down into the Pit of Hell, to spend Eternity in torments of Hellfire and Brimstone.

My Mam says that she's already in bloody torments from Virgy going on at her, and Hell will be a welcome release.

Whenever my Mam swears, Virgy always goes down on her knees and prays for her salvation. She keeps saying,

"Forgive this sinful woman, Lord, she knows not what she does! Please make her whiter than the driven snow."

"I'll tan your backside blacker than the driven soot if you don't stop playing me up, my wench," my Mam tells her.

When Uncle Sid goes to the pub, Virgy follows him with some of her mates from the Band of Hope. They've made some big cardboard banners with 'Down with Demon Drink' written on them, and they parades up and down outside the pub doors all the time Uncle Sid is inside. Virgy's got a box that she stands on, and she shouts to everybody who passes by, and when they stops to listen she tells them, "My Uncle Sid is in that pub swilling down the drink, and we're all starving at home. He doesn't buy us any food, he spends all his money on the Demon Rum."

And all the old women says, "Oh what a shame! Oh, the poor little soul!" And they shouts into the pub at Uncle Sid, "You ought to be ashamed of yourself, you wicked drunken bugger."

After a bit the landlord always tells Uncle Sid, "I can't serve you any more drink while that girl and her gang are parading up and down like this. You'll have to go, because she's ruining my trade."

Uncle Sid goes mad then and comes out to tell Virgy to bugger off and leave him alone. But Virgy don't listen, she only shouts, "Praise the Lord, we have saved this miserable sinner. Praise the Lord!"

Uncle Sid told my Mam that every pub within a day's march of our house has threatened to give him his ticket because of our Virgy and her gang. He says that if Virgy don't leave him in peace to have a quiet drink he's going to bloody well strangle her and all her mates as well.

When he says that my Mam tells him, "You lay a finger on my precious girl and I'll bloody swing for you."

Uncle Sid has never laid a finger on me or our Virgy anyway. He just sulks with us when we plays him up too much.

Last Saturday when the pubs opened Uncle Sid asked me to do him a favour. "Go and look in the street and see if Virgy and her gang are out there waiting for me," He said, and he give me a sixpence.

Virgy wasn't in the street, but Shirley MacDowd was standing on the corner of West Street. Shirley MacDowd is our Virgy's best friend. I don't like her, she's horrible, and she's got droopy drawers as well.

"Virgy's best friend is down on the corner of West Street," I told my Uncle Sid, and he looked ever so sly.

"Right then," he said. "I'm going to have to use my Secret Service training. I knew it would come in useful one day."

"I didn't know that you was in the Secret Service, Uncle Sid?"

"Of course you didn't know, Specs. If you had of known, then it wouldn't be secret, would it? When I was in the Secret Service I was known as a master of disguise. The Jerries called me 'The Man of a Thousand Faces'. They could never catch me, even when I was operating right under their very noses in Adolf Hitler's headquarters."

"Can you tell me some stories about what you was doing, Uncle Sid," I said.

"Someday, Specs, I'll tell you the full story of my

exploits behind the enemy lines. But that can only be when the war is over. I'm bound to silence by the Official Secrets Act until then."

Uncle Sid let me watch him putting his disguise on. He put on a big trilby hat that used to be my real Dad's. And Uncle Harold's old Home Guard coat which reached right down to his ankles, and he put on a pair of sunglasses. He turned the coat collar up and pulled the hat down over his head like a gangster.

"There now, Specs, you wouldn't be able to recognise me if you met me walking down the street, would you? Didn't I tell you that I was a master of disguise?"

When he was all disguised my Mam come in and asked him, "What the bloody hell are you playing at? It's boiling hot outside. You'll get heat-stroke if you goes out wearing that lot. There's only you and Filthy Charlie who'd be daft enough to wear army overcoats today."

"Oh is that so!" Uncle Sid got all snotty. "Well it's your bloody daughter's fault that I've got to dress like Filthy Charlie. It's the only way I can go and get a quiet drink without her and her gang of bloody rotten angels chasing after me."

After I had another look outside to see if the coast was clear Uncle Sid snuck out of the house and went up the street away from Shirley MacDowd.

"Hilda, come and have a look at this silly daft sod!" my Mam shouted, and her and Hilda stuck their heads out of the window to watch Uncle Sid, and they kept on laughing.

"Just look at him, will you," my Mam kept on saying. "What the bloody hell does he think he's doing?"

"He's doing what he used to do behind the enemy

lines, when he was in the Secret Service," I told them. "Not even Adolf Hitler could catch him. He's the man of a thousand faces."

Uncle Sid looked ever so good, the way he was ducking behind walls, and peeping round the corners, and then running to hide in the next entry, it was just like he was on the pictures.

Then our Virgy and her droopy drawers mates come home with all their banners; and when Virgy found out that Uncle Sid had escaped they all run to look for him. So I run ever so fast to catch Uncle Sid up and told him that they was looking for him.

"I'm not bothered," he said, ever so scornful. "My disguise will fool that lot."

Just as he said that Virgy and her gang come round the bottom corner, and Virgy shouted, "There he is!" And they all started hooting and screeching.

Uncle Sid run for it, and when he went round the next corner he ducked into a dark entry to hide.

Two women was standing by the dark entry when Uncle Sid run up it, and I heard one of them say, "I reckon that's that flasher what's been hanging about round here. He's wearing a big hat and a long coat like he was wearing when he showed his Wotsit to our Cynthia the day before yesterday."

There was a copper coming down the road and the women went up to him, and they was waving their arms about and kept on pointing to the dark entry.

The copper come up to the entry and he said, "Come on out of there you. The game's up!"

Uncle Sid never come out, so the copper went down the entry and pulled him out of it, and the two women was shouting, "That's him, constable. That's the flasher!"

"Now officer, if you'll just let me explain. This is all a terrible mistake," Uncle Sid kept on saying. But the copper only dragged him along, and kept on telling him, "You can explain down at the station. You're under arrest."

Virgy and her gang ran up the street then, and Virgy told Uncle Sid, "There you are, Uncle Sid. I told you that you'd get into trouble if you kept on sinning, didn't I."

The copper asked Virgy, "Do you know this man, my duck?"

Virgy was nodding. "Yes, we all knows him, don't we girls. He's a wicked sinner."

And all her gang was nodding and telling the copper, "Yes, we knows him. He's called Uncle Sid and he's a wicked sinner."

"There now, do you hear that?" The copper got ever so red in the face, and he shook Uncle Sid by the collar 'til his head rattled backwards and forwards. "Even these innocent little children knows you, don't they, you filthy beast!"

"Oh my God! This is all a terrible mistake, officer!" Uncle Sid was moaning, "It's all a terrible mistake. Oh my God!"

Then he saw me and he told me, "Tell him, Specs. Tell him who I am." Then the copper asked me. "Do you know this man, as well?"

"Yes, he's Uncle Sid," I told him. "And he gave me sixpence to keep a lookout for those girls."

The copper's face got even redder then, and he shook Uncle Sid's collar until Uncle Sid's teeth was rattling.

"So, you're involving this poor little lad in your filthy

94

schemes as well are you? Just wait 'til I get you in the station, my bucko. I'll learn you a lesson."

"Oh my God! Oh my God!" Uncle Sid was moaning and groaning. "Oh my God!"

"You come along to the police station, son. And you ladies," the copper told me and the two women.

"Can we come as well?" Virgy asked.

But the copper told her no, she wouldn't be needed. But her and her gang come along anyway. It was just like a procession with us all marching behind the copper and Uncle Sid. And when we turned the corner we met Uncle Harold coming home from the cemetery.

He likes to go there and sit among the grave-stones. He says it always cheers him up.

"Oh, thank God!" Uncle Sid cried out. "Harold, Harold, tell the officer who I am."

Uncle Harold looked all snotty at him, and he said very scornful like, "Yes, I know who you are, Sidney Tompkin. And I know what you are as well. You're a murderer. A murderer of innocent little creatures. That's what you are." And he told the copper, "You've got the right man there, Officer. I'll be a witness against him for what he was going to do."

The copper was looking really excited now, and his face was really really red. "What was he planning to do, Sir?" Yeh, that's what he called Uncle Harold, he called him 'Sir'!

"He's going to murder them and eat them. All those poor little innocent souls. He's got them locked up in a cage in his back garden. You've got to save them, Officer. you've got to save those poor little innocent souls." Uncle Harold got all upset then, and started to cry.

"Don't you worry, Sir. I'll save them," The copper told him. "I'll have to ask you to accompany me and the prisoner to the police station to give us a statement concerning the prisoner."

So I took Uncle Harold by his hand and brought him along with us. I have to lead him by the hand when he's crying because his glasses gets all steamed up when he cries and he can't see where he's walking then.

Johnny Merry and Terry Murtagh and Fatty Polson saw us, and they come running to ask me what was going on. I told them that Uncle Sid had been arrested because he was the 'flasher' who'd shown his Wotsit to Cynthia Gould the day before yesterday.

"What's a Wotsit?" Fatty Polson wanted to know.

I didn't know myself, but Johnny Merry said it was the posh word for your willie.

I was scared then, because I didn't know before that you could get took to the police station if your showed your willie to somebody.

Johnny Merry got scared as well, because the other day me and Johnny Merry and Carol Perks all went down the lane and we showed each other our willies. Terry Murtagh was scared as well, because him and his sisters are always showing each other their willies, and Fatty Polson has showed his willie to Terry Murtagh's sisters as well.

"Don't tell the coppers about what we did in the lane, Specs," Johnny Merry told me. "Or we'll be locked up with your Uncle Sid."

The three of them all run away then, and I wanted to run away as well, but I couldn't because Uncle Harold had ever such a tight hold of my hand.

When we got to the police station we all went inside

and a sergeant copper behind the counter asked, "Who's this then? I hope it's not another bloody Jerry paratrooper. I've got a cupboard full of nuns' clothes and tommy-guns already."

"No, Sarge, this is something big," the copper who had hold of Uncle Sid told him. "I reckon we've got another Jack the Ripper here."

"He's worse than Jack the Ripper," Uncle Harold shouted. "He's a slaughterer of poor little innocents."

"All right, Sir, just calm down now," the sergeant said. "I'll take your statement in a minute. Lock this man up until I'm ready for him." They dragged Uncle Sid off to the cells then and he kept on shouting, "Oh, my God, this is all a terrible mistake! Tell them, Specs! Tell them, Harold! Somebody tell them!"

The sergeant copper took Uncle Harold into another room then, but they let him wipe his glasses first so that he could see where he was walking.

Virgy and her gang started singing hymns, and a copper told them to stop making such a racket. Virgy knelt down and prayed: "Oh Lord, forgive this miserable sinner, for he knows not what he's doing."

The copper got mad then and chased her and her gang away out of the station. Then I heard the sergeant copper shouting "Rabbits? Bloody rabbits!"

And the next minute Uncle Harold come out of the room looking all upset, and the sergeant copper come out after him telling him, "Now just bugger off out of my sight, you, or I'll have you nicked for wasting police time."

Then he said to me, "And what's your story?"

So I told him that Uncle Sid wanted to go to the pub without Virgy and her gang chasing after him, and he'd

97

give me a tanner to keep a lookout for them so he could sneak away. And that he'd only run up the dark entry to hide from them.

Cynthia Gould come then looking for her Mam, and the sergeant copper told her, "I want you to have a look at a man, and see if you recognise him."

He took her down to see Uncle Sid, and she said that Uncle Sid wasn't the flasher. So he set him free.

Uncle Sid was all white and trembling when we got outside the police station. "My God, Specs, I need a drink!" He kept on saying. "I need a stiff drink."

The first pub we came to he looked all around to see if our Virgy was there, but she wasn't, so he said, "Tell your Mam I'll be home when the pub's shut, Specs." And he went inside.

When I got home Virgy and her gang were there telling my Mam and Hilda what had happened, and they was laughing about it. Then my Mam asked me where Uncle Sid was now, and I told her that he was in the pub by the police station.

"Come on, gang," our Virgy screeched, "We must save his soul." And they all ran off with their banners.

I couldn't help but feel all sorrowful for Uncle Sid then . . .

Chapter Eighteen

We had 'Woolton Pie' for our dinner today. It was horrible, all parsnips and potatoes, and my Mam made something she called 'Carrot Croquettes' to eat with the Woolton Pie. They was horrible as well. But my Mam said that if me and Virgy didn't eat up every bit then Lord Woolton would come and get us. She's always saying that Lord Woolton will come and get us if we don't eat the crusts when we has a piece of bread and jam, or if we leaves anything on our plates.

Lord Woolton lives in a big palace in London, and he gives everybody in the country their food. He talks to us sometimes on the wireless, but I've never seen him down town. Johnny Merry has seen him though. He says that Lord Woolton come down the street late one night when everybody was in bed, and he come to Johnny Merry's house and asked him what he thought about the food ration. Johnny Merry says that he told Lord Woolton to give us a lot more sweets and chocolate on the ration, and he says that Lord Woolton promised that he would after next Christmas. Johnny Merry says that Lord Woolton was wearing a big cloak and hat, and he was riding in a gold coach with four horses pulling it.

I wish Lord Woolton would come to our house, because

then I'd tell him to give us oranges and bananas and melons and pineapples and peaches and coconuts. I don't know what a melon tastes like, or a pineapple or coconut or a peach, but I've tasted the others and they're ever so nice. My Mam says melons and pineapples and peaches are lovely, and that you can drink milk from a coconut and that's lovely as well.

The grown-ups talk about food a lot. They keep on telling each other about all the wonderful meals they used to eat before the war.

I only really like chips though. From Colley's chip shop down the Hill. I should like to eat them all the time. Whenever I get thruppence to spare I always go to Colley's chip shop and I buy thruppence worth of chips with scratchings. I put a lot of vinegar and salt on them and eat them very slow so they last a long time. They're lovely.

I like eating sugar as well. When there's nobody about I go into our pantry and I eat some sugar from the bowl. Another thing I like to eat sometimes is an onion. Mr Stanton who's got the shop round the corner gives me a big onion sometimes, but I have to eat it in front of him and the people in his shop. They all pulls faces when I'm eating it, and Mr Stanton keeps on saying, "God strike me down dead, how can you eat that, son?" And he tells the other people, "You wouldn't believe it if you couldn't see it, would you!"

I don't like tinned eggs though. But every fortnight my Mam gets some fresh eggs on the ration. She gets one egg for each of us, and she makes ever such a fuss of them. She gave me one once, but I didn't like it, so now Virgy has my egg as well as her own. I don't like Spam either. It's all rubbery.

At school they gives us milk and orange juice and cod liver oil. The orange juice is horrible and sour, and they gives us the milk after we've ate the cod liver oil, so the milk tastes nasty as well. Whenever any of the kids pulls a face about the nasty taste Miss Brown always tells them, "Stop making such a fuss. The King and Queen and the Princesses don't pull a face when they have their cod liver oil. They swallow it with a smile, because they know that it's so good for them."

"I bet they has sugar with theirs though, Miss," Johnny Merry said one day. "They has lots and lots of sugar to eat because they're not on the ration books like us."

Miss Brown got all snotty with him. She always gets snotty with Johnny Merry, whatever he says.

"Who told you that, Merry?" she asked him in her sour voice. Miss Brown's got different voices you know. She's got a sweet voice when she talks to Aubrey Jones-Evans and Rita Spencer and their gang, and she's got a sour voice when she talks to me and Johnny Merry and our gang.

"Our Doreen told me." Johnny Merry arn't fritted of Miss Brown's sour voice. "And our Doreen told me as well that the Royal Family lives on the fat of the land, and not on the ration like us," he said.

"Just for your information, Merry, let me tell you that our Royal Family eat exactly the same rations as all the rest of us." Miss Brown was looking daggers at him. "And your sister Doreen should be careful what she says. She could get into serious trouble telling such lies."

"Phooo! Our Doreen don't give a bugger what she says," Johnny Merry told her. And then Miss Brown clouted him for swearing, so he shut up.

Anyway, tomorrow we're going to have rabbit stew in our house, made with one of our own rabbits.

It's the first time that we're going to eat one of our own rabbits. We had to wait 'til now for it to grow big enough. Uncle Sid is going to kill it and skin it before he goes to work, and my Mam is going to cook it. Uncle Harold says that he's not going to eat any of it because he would feel like a cannibal eating one of his little bunny friends. But Hilda says that if Uncle Harold is going to be such a silly daft sod then she'll have his share. Granny Smith says that she'll only be able to manage to drink a bit of the gravy, because her last tooth has just fell out so she can't chew anything hard. Uncle Sid went mad when she said that, because he reckons that the rabbit meat will melt in our mouths. He says that it will be so sweet and tender we won't have to chew it, only suck it.

Our Virgy hasn't said anything about it at all. She's too busy building a holy shrine in our backyard. Her and her gang have pinched a lot of old bricks from the bombed houses and they're building a 'Holy Shrine of the Virgin Mary'.

Virgy says that when she was coming out of the lav the other night she saw a vision of the Virgin Mary standing on the old mangle that's in the corner of the backyard. Her and her gang spent all the next day kneeling and praying in front of the mangle. Uncle Sid didn't half moan about them being there, because he said he couldn't even go for a pee without falling over a load of bloody kids. And he said that he couldn't concentrate on the football results when he was sat on the lav because of the racket Virgy and her gang was kicking up, screeching and wailing to the Lord to send them another vision.

102

This afternoon Virgy told my Mam that the Virgin Mary had chosen our backyard to come to because our family were such hardened sinners and they must be redeemed in the Blood of the Lamb.

When Virgy said that, my Mam just clucked her tongue and shook her head, then stared up at the ceiling for a long long time. Until our Virgy asked her, "Can you see her as well, Mam?"

"See who?" My Mam said.

"Our Blessed Lady," Virgy told her. "She's standing next to the light bulb."

My Mam sent Virgy to bed then, and when Hilda come home she told her, "I'm going to have that silly little cow put away if she sees any more visions, because she's driving me bloody well mad!"

It would be ever so good if my Mam did have our Virgy put away, because then I'd have the bed all to myself. It's horrible sleeping with our Virgy, because she keeps getting up all night to go and look out of the window to see if the Virgin Mary is standing on the mangle again, and every time she gets up she wakes me up as well. It arn't fair!

Chapter Nineteen

We all got up early today because Uncle Sid was going to kill the rabbit before he went to work. Shirley MacDowd, our Virgy's best friend, come round as well. "What does you want?" I asked her.

"Mind your own business, Four Eyes," she told me.

"Maaammm, our Specs is being horrible to Shirley and calling her rude names!" our Virgy screeched.

"Specs, I'll bloody tan your backside for you if you don't behave yourself and leave the girls alone!" my Mam shouted out of the window. "Now get in here."

My Mam always believes Virgy instead of me, so I just kept quiet and went back inside the house and the two girls was sticking their tongues out at me. I don't like them two. They're both horrible.

Uncle Sid was sitting in the back kitchen having a cup of tea, and Hilda come downstairs to tell my Mam, "Harold's really upset about this rabbit being killed, you know, Effie. He's sobbing his heart out upstairs."

Uncle Sid grinned and said ever so nasty-like, "I don't think he's crying about the rabbit, you know, Hilda. He's crying because it's just been announced by the government that they're going to make every man in this country do some war work."

"Oh, very funny, I'm sure!" Hilda said, all snotty.

"How are you going to kill the rabbit, Uncle Sid?" I asked him.

"I shall kill it the way I used to kill Jerry sentries when I was in the Commandos," he told me. "I shall grab it from behind and, using ju-jitsu, I shall break its neck."

"Will it hurt it?"

"Nooo, Specs, it won't feel a thing. Silent instant killing, that's what I was trained to do. In the Commandos I was known as 'The Cobra' because I was so deadly and silent, and struck so fast. The Jerries was fritted to death of me when I was raiding the enemy coast. Winston Churchill reckoned I was worth a division of soldiers to the war effort, because wherever I was operating the Jerries used to have to move up a Panzer division so that the Jerry sentries could hide inside the tanks, because they was too terrified to be outside by themselves when they knew that 'The Cobra' was coming."

My Mam give him her look and told him, "I reckon they used to call you the 'Slow Worm', more like."

He stared ever so fierce at her. "Let me tell you, that someday Sidney Tompkin's name is going to be known all over the Empire for what he did in this war. Just you wait 'til I'm allowed to tell my story. You'll be sorry you doubted me then, but it'll be too late, because I'll probably be dead by then."

"Why, Uncle Sid? Why will you be dead?" I asked.

He looked very solemn and sad then, and he told me, "Because, Specs, a man who's suffered what I has suffered in the service of his country can never live to be old. My body has endured too much."

"Will you give over your bloody nonsense and get that

bloody rabbit killed and skinned so I can start cooking it."
My Mam told him very sharp.

"All right, all right, let me just finish me cup of tea,
will you, woman!"

"Can I come and watch you do it, Uncle Sid?"

"No, Specs. You're too young to see violent death
inflicted. It'll only give you nightmares."

"No it won't, Uncle Sid. I saw Tarzan kill twenty
Blackies on the pictures last week. And the week before
I saw Errol Flynn kill hundreds of Jerries."

"That's only pretend stuff, Specs. This is the real thing
what I'm going to do to the rabbit."

"Oh, go on, Uncle Sid! Let me watch."

"Tell him, will you, Effie."

"If Uncle Sid says no, then it's no. So just shut up
your whining and pestering, or I'll give you summat to
whine about."

I didn't say anything then. Because I knew a place
where I could hide and watch Uncle Sid kill the rabbit.
After a bit I told my Mam, "I'm going out to get some
dandelions."

In the backyard Virgy and Shirley MacDowd was
kneeling in front of the 'Holy Shrine'. All it is is a
stack of bricks and Virgy's old doll standing on top of
the mangle with a bit of rag wrapped round its head and
a cardboard halo pinned to its neck. They've put some
jam-jars with flowers all round it as well, and a candle
that my Mam give them in front of it.

"What's you doing, Virgy?" my Mam shouted out of
the window.

"We're praying for the poor little rabbit's soul, and that
God will forgive Uncle Sid for murdering it."

"That bloody daughter of yours will drive me bloody potty!" Uncle Sid grumbled. But my Mam only laughed.

I went and hid, and waited until Uncle Sid come out the house.

Granny Smith poked her head out from the upstairs window and shouted, "Can you see them bloody Jerries, Sidney? The noisy buggers has just woke me up again. I'll give them a smack in the chops if I comes down there."

Granny Smith is having one of her funny turns again. It's lasted for ages now.

Mrs Masters leaned out from her upstairs window as well and shouted, "You're nothing but a gallant fool, Jungle Jim. Those rabbits are savage beasts, they've killed the last ten men who went after them. You'll never come back alive." And she roared with laughing.

Uncle Sid never even looked up at her, he was walking ever so proud and tall, just like Hopalong Cassidy was last week when he went to face the fastest gunfighter West of the Pecos. It's ever such a good serial, I can't wait 'til Saturday to see if Hopalong kills the fastest gunfighter. I expect he will though, because there's still five weeks for the serial to run, so Hopalong can't get killed yet can he!

When the rabbits saw Uncle Sid coming they all come crowding to the front of their hutch to see if he'd brought them any dandelions.

The nearer Uncle Sid got to the hutches, the slower he was walking. His face was ever so pale and white and sweaty, and he stopped about five yards away from the hutches and stood looking at the rabbits for ages, He stood there for so long I got tired of hiding and I come out and said, "What's the matter, Uncle Sid?"

He shouted out and jumped right up in the air. Then when he saw it was me he didn't half tell me off.

"You've bloody well messed everything up now, Specs. I'd just selected my target and now you've ruined it. The bloody rabbits knows that I'm coming now. All the element of surprise is gone."

"Well, you can still get hold of it, Uncle Sid. You can easy reach into the hutch and grab it."

"Don't talk so daft. If I have to grab it like that all the meat will turn sour. The whole secret of having sweet and tender meat is to kill the rabbit when it's off its guard. My Christ, but you're stupid sometimes, you are, Specs."

He was acting all disgusted now. "Phooo, I'll just have to leave it now, and it's all your fault that we've got nothing for our dinner."

"Why is it my fault?" I wanted to know.

"Because you've give the game away to the bloody rabbit, that's why it's your fault."

He went storming off up the garden, swearing and carrying on about me, and when he went into the house I could hear him shouting to my Mam about what I'd done.

I thought that I'd better keep out of the way for a bit, because I'd get a tanning from my Mam for spoiling her dinner, so I run up the entry and down the street. I met Johnny Merry coming to call for me then, and when I told him what had happened he said, "Phooo, me and you can kill a rabbit for your Mam's dinner. It's easy."

"How shall we kill it?"

"We'll play our 'Robin Hood' game. We'll make bows and arrows and shoot it. It'll be ever such a good game, Specs. We'll let the rabbits out into the garden and they can be the 'King's Deer'. We'll charge up on them like Robin Hood does and we'll kill them with our bows and arrows. They won't know we're coming to kill them, will they? They'll think that we're only playing. So the meat will be nice then. And you won't get into trouble with your Mam this time, because she wants the rabbit killed, don't she?"

We used to make our cat the 'King's Deer' when we played 'Robin Hood'. But one day Virgy saw us and she told my Mam, and I got a tanning for shooting arrows at our cat, and my Mam said if I ever did it again she'd have me put away for being cruel to animals. So we don't play 'Robin Hood' with our cat any more.

We snuck down round the back of the Hostel, because there's a tree there growing up by the back wall of the Hostel that's got good bow sticks on it. There's a shed and greenhouse there as well by the back door, where we gets our arrows and string. We makes the arrows from thin canes, and we sticks a nail in one end for a point. We gets the nails from the Hostel shed as well. There's a big box full of rusty nails there.

Old Mr Smout does the Hostel gardens. He has to wear glasses like I does, only his are ever so thick and one side of them has got a black patch on it. He can't hardly see anything at all. When we're scrumpin' we just keeps very still when he comes down the garden, and he walks right by us because he can't see us hiding.

Sometimes we plays 'Jungle Patrol' with him. He's the Japs and we're the Chindits. That's ever such a good game. We hides in the bushes and waits for him to come past, then we ambushes him and chucks things at him and crawls through the bushes like Chindits, and he keeps on swearing and shouting, "I can see you, you little buggers! I knows who you am! I'll tell your Dads and Mams on you."

And we laughs because we knows that he can't see us, and he don't know who we are.

When we went to get our bows and arrows we saw Mr Smout down the very bottom of the gardens, and I wanted to play 'Jungle Patrol', but Johnny Merry said, "No, we can play Jungle Patrol any time can't we? But we might not be able to play Robin Hood again this week. Not with real live Kings Deer."

We went to the shed and got our arrows and nails and string and took them and hid them in the bushes. Then we went back and got the hacksaw from the bench, and then we crept up to the tree. Johnny Merry told me to keep the lookout and then he climbed right up to the top branches where the good bow sticks are and started to saw.

He cut two good ones and dropped them down to me, then when he was climbing back down he stopped and stared into the upstairs window. He waved to me to come up, and he was grinning all over his face. When I climbed up he whispered, "Look in there."

The window was open and we could see through it. There was a big bed and a man and a woman was laying on the bed, and they was having a Doo. It was a couple of minutes before I knew who they was, because Miss Mason hadn't got her glasses on, and Rodney hadn't got his deer-stalker hat and plus-fours on.

They was both bare, and Rodney was laying on top of Miss Mason and bouncing up and down on her. Every time he bounced Miss Mason was gasping out, "Rodney, Rodney, Rodney, Rodney . . . !"

And he was gasping out, "Gracie, Gracie, Gracie, Gracie . . . !"

Me and Johnny Merry was laughing, and we wished we'd got our bows and arrows with us, then we could have shot Rodney right up his big fat bum.

While we was watching Rodney started to bounce faster and faster, and higher and higher, and he was gasping ever so loud, "GRACIE, GRACIE GRACIE GRACIE . . . !"

And Miss Mason was squealing, "RODNEY RODNEY RODNEY RODNEY . . . !"

And we was laughing and laughing.

And then all of a sudden Rodney give a big shout and he flopped down still, and he groaned out.

"Ohhhhh, Gracie . . . !"

And Miss Mason groaned out, "Ohhhhh, Rodney."

And Johnny Merry shouted out ever so loud, "REMEMBER YOUR HEART RODNEY! THINK OF YOUR HEART!"

Miss Mason screamed and Rodney fell off the bed. And me and Johnny Merry shot down the tree and grabbed our bowsticks and escaped. But we was laughing so much that I fell into a raspberry bush and scratched all me arms and legs and face.

We stayed hid in the bushes until the coast was all clear. But we didn't mind hiding because we made our bows and arrows while we was in there.

When we got back to my house there was nobody there except for Granny Smith, and she was sleeping on the sofa in the front room.

Me and Johnny Merry was fighting about who was going to be Robin Hood and who was going to be Little

John. In the end I was Robin Hood, because the rabbits are Uncle Sid's and they lives at my house.

We opened both the hutches and then went to the top of the back garden to let the rabbits come out. When they was all hopping about the garden, we started to play.

"Look, Little John, there are the 'King's Deer'. Is there any sign of the Sheriff of Nottingham?"

"No, Robin. The Sheriff of Nottingham is in his castle."

"OK then, Little John. Let's hunt the 'King's Deer' and we'll give the meat to the poor."

"OK Robin, let's go!"

We shouted our battle-cries and charged.

The rabbits all run off ever so fast before we could even get a shot at them. They was all over the neighbour's gardens and backyards, and some of them run out into the street. We charged after them, shouting our battle-cries.

It was a smashing game. We never managed to hit a single rabbit with our arrows, but we had ever such a lot of near misses.

We was having a rest, and Aubrey, the posh kid, come to tell us, "My mother says that if you don't come and fetch your rabbits from out of our garden immediately, she's going to fetch a policeman to you. Your rabbits are eating all our lettuces.

"Bugger off!" Johnny Merry told him, and shot an arrow at him. The arrow stuck right into Aubrey's leg, and he didn't half screech, and he run home with the arrow dangling down in his leg. The next minute Mrs Jones-Evans come roaring and screeching out of her house and me and Johnny Merry didn't half run fast.

I was hiding under the bed when my Mam found me. She didn't half give me a tanning. Well, I got two tannings really. One was for letting the rabbits out and the other was for shooting the arrow into Aubrey's leg.

I never shot the arrow into Aubrey's leg, did I. It was Johnny Merry did that. Johnny Merry never gets a tanning, does he. It arn't fair!

Uncle Sid is still outside trying to catch the rabbits. But he hasn't managed to catch a single one of them yet. I bet I'll get another tanning off my Mam for that as well.

It arn't fair!

Chapter Twenty

All the neighbours are carrying on about Uncle Sid's rabbits. Mr Griffiths says that they've burrowed under his lawn and that there's holes all over it now where the burrows has caved in. The rabbits has ate all Mrs Savin's flowers, and Mrs Jones-Evans says that they've ate all her salad and herb garden and has caused hundreds of pounds worth of damage to her rare Asiatic rhododendron bushes that she had specially imported from India. Even Miss Freeman is mad because the rabbits has ate the bark off her lilac tree, and she says that the tree might die now.

Uncle Sid arn't sulking with me for letting the rabbits out though. All he says is, "Do you know something, Specs? Every time I look at you and think of my rabbits I just want to weep."

He goes out chasing the rabbits every night after he comes home from work, but so far he arn't caught a single one. He reckons that if he don't catch any of them by the end of the week, then he's going to borrow a machine-gun from the Home Guards and shoot them.

Hilda was ever so nasty to him when he said that.

"That's just about your bloody drop, arn't it," she told him, all scornful-like. "Using a bloody machine-gun to shoot poor little critters who're only doing what comes natural to them. You're the cruellest man I've ever met, killing such harmless little things."

"Cruel? Me cruel?" Uncle Sid was all indignant. "You was willing enough to eat the bloody things, wasn't you, and they'd have to be killed if you was going to eat them, wouldn't they. Or was you thinking of eating them alive?"

"That's different," Hilda told him, "because they was going to have a painless death before Effie cooked them, wasn't they? Not be used as targets for bloody machine-guns."

Uncle Harold hasn't said anything about the machine-gun though. Because he's had a terrible shock. The man at the Labour Exchange has told him that he's put his name down for a 'Bevin Boy'. That means that he'll have to go down a coal mine and dig coal.

Uncle Harold says that if God had wanted him to go down dark tunnels he would have made him a mole and not a flower of the sun like he is. Hilda is really upset about it as well. She says that the man at the Labour Exchange is being spiteful because everybody knows that Uncle Harold is too delicate to do nasty dirty work like coal mining.

When my Mam found out that they was going to send Uncle Harold down the coal mine she laughed and said that she'd write to Mr Bevin and tell him that Uncle Harold won't be any use down the mine, because he's too fritted of the dark.

It's true you know, Uncle Harold is fritted of the dark. I know that because he always has to have a night light burning when he's in bed. Even though Hilda is there with him to keep him company.

116

I don't have any night lights when I'm in bed, because I'm not fritted of the dark at all. Neither is Uncle Sid.

Uncle Sid says that when he was a Chindit fighting the Japs in the jungle, he used to love the dark, because he said it was his best friend. He says that all the Japs are fritted of the dark, and that he used to creep right into their camp on the dark nights and frighten them to death by pretending that he was a ghost. He said that the Japs called him the 'White Phantom from Hell'.

When my Mam heard him say that she told him, "It's a pity that those rabbits arn't Japanese, then you could creep around the gardens tonight and frighten them all to death, and then we might get a bit of peace from the neighbours."

Today my Mam had an idea about how to save Uncle Harold from being a Bevin Boy. She reckons that if he could find a job in the town, then the man at the Labour Exchange wouldn't make him go down the coal mine.

"Find a job in the town?" Uncle Sid said all scornful. "Who in their right minds would give that bloody sunflower a job?" Then he laughed very nasty-like and said, "Mind you, there's one job he could do, when you comes to think about it. He could sit on one of the tombstones down in the cemetery and pretend he was a statue. That ought to suit him down to the ground, because he likes the cemetery don't he, and he wouldn't have to do anything at all except sit on his backside all day."

"You've just give me an idea," my Mam told him. "I was talking to Smiling Sam the other day, and he told me that he wanted a bloke to help him with the funerals."

'Smiling Sam' is what they calls the undertaker. 'Smiling

117

Sam the Coffin Man'. He's always laughing and singing and whistling and he tells everybody that he's the jolliest undertaker in the whole of Christendom.

There's one song that he likes the best, and he keeps on singing it. It goes:

> *You may roam this world,*
> *You may drink your drink,*
> *You may eat your meat,*
> *And kiss girls so sweet.*
> *You may laugh and play*
> *With never a care.*
> *But I'll nail you in the end . . .*

Every time he comes up our street he stops people and tells them, "It's a pity that you aren't ready to die this week, because I could give you a special bargain price on a spare coffin I've got in the shop. I made it for Old Thomas down Bodley Road, but the bugger's still breathing, so I'm stuck with it."

Another thing he always asks is, "What's the difference between me and a Chinese laundryman? Well, the Chink stiffens the collars, and I collars the stiff 'uns."

Then he roars with laughing and takes out his ruler and measures us up, and tells us, "Yes, I could give you a good bargain price on a nice bit of oak that I've got in the shop. It would fit you a treat."

But Smiling Sam's wife is ever so sour and miserable. My Mam says that her face would curdle the cream while it's still in the cow. She stutters when she talks so everybody calls her 'K'K'K'K'Katie K'K'K'K'Koffin.'

Anyway, when Uncle Harold come home from the

118

cemetery my Mam said, "Get your best bib and tucker on, Harold. You and me are going down to see Smiling Sam about a job for you."

"A job? For me?" Uncle Harold didn't seem pleased at all. He looked just like he looked on the day when he left his best coat on the sofa and our cat had some kittens on it.

My Mam got a bit snotty with him. "Well, you either get a job with Smiling Sam, or you go down the coal mine, so suit yourself."

He still looked miserable, and my Mam coaxed him a bit.

"Look, our Harold, you know how much you likes to go down to the cemetery. Well, if you works for Smiling Sam you'll be able to go down there all the time, and get paid for it."

He cheered up a bit then. "I hadn't thought about it like that, Effie."

So he put his best clothes on and his bowler hat and they went off to see Smiling Sam. When they come back they was both all happy and smiling.

We was all having our supper, and my Mam told us, "Harold starts work tomorrow for Smiling Sam. He's going to be the 'Mute'. He's going to wear a posh top hat and a tailcoat and walk in front of the hearse."

"He'll have to look all sad and solemn when he does that, won't he," Hilda said.

"That'll be easy for him," Uncle Sid said. "All he needs to do is to keep on thinking about work. You know how much that depresses him."

There was a knocking on the front door then and when my Mam opened it there was a crowd of old women there, and a big fat priest who was carrying a great big wooden cross.

"Yes, what can I do for you?" she asked them.

"We're the Sodality of the Blessed martyr, Saint Sharon of Basildon," the big fat priest told her. "And we've come on a pilgrimage to this Holy Shrine."

"Hallelujah! Hallelujah! Hallelujah!" the old women all kept shouting.

"Well you've come to the wrong place, your Reverence," my Mam told him.

"No we haven't, my child. This is number 31 isn't it? Your daughter Virginia wrote to us and invited us here. And you must call me 'Father'."

"Who's at the door, Effie?" Granny Smith shouted. She's still having one of her funny turns, you know.

"It's Father," My Mam told her.

"Jesus Christ! It's a miracle!" Granny Smith got all excited. "The bugger's been dead and buried for twenty-five years. Have they dug him up, or what? How is he looking?"

"He's looking very well," my Mam said.

"Ahhrr, trust that bugger to take good care of himself. Well you can tell him to sod off. He's not creeping back into my bed. I like being a virgin."

The priest was looking all shocked then and my Mam started to laugh and the old women kept on shouting, "Hallelujah! Hallelujah! Hallelujah!"

Some of the neighbours was looking out of their windows and moaning about the noise, so my Mam told the priest, "The only shrine here is the one my daughter and her gang built on our old mangle in our backyard."

"That's the one we're looking for, my child." The

120

priest was ever so happy then. "Your daughter is a little saint and we'd like to see her as well and hear from her own lips the story of the wonderful vision she saw."

"Hallelujah! Hallelujah! Hallelujah!" the old women shouted.

"I wish you'd keep that bloody noise down!" one of the neighbours was screeching. "We can't hear ourselves think with all this bloody racket going on."

All of a sudden, Uncle Sid put his oar in. He come rushing to the front door and he was all false and sugary. "Please follow me, your Reverence," he was bowing to the priest and rubbing his hands together, "and you ladies, please all follow me."

He took all of them down the entry and round into our backyard. "Could I please ask you all to remember that this is Holy Ground, so please could you all be very very quiet," he told them, and then he come back inside the house.

When they got into the backyard our Virgy was kneeling in front of the 'Holy Shrine' like she does every night.

"Oh, how sweet!"

"Isn't she adorable!"

"Oh, just look at that sainted child!"

The old women was all cooing and smiling at our Virgy, and our Virgy was wearing her 'Holy Face'. That's when she stares up at her old doll with big wide eyes and keeps on smiling and nodding at it.

They all said some prayers then, and sang some hymns, and when they was finished they all started to put money on the old mangle. We was all watching from the back kitchen window and Uncle Sid was chuckling and rubbing his hands together.

My Mam said, "I wonder what they're doing that for? Putting money on the mangle?"

"Shush!" Uncle Sid told her. "That's why I took them around the back. I knew they'd give donations. If we boxes clever I reckon that we'll make our bloody fortunes with this shrine, Effie. We'll have to start selling 'Holy Relics' of course, and postcards and souvenirs. Let's get that busted floorboard down from the attic before they all goes. We'll cut bits off it and tell them that it's bits of the 'True Cross'. I reckon we can charge a quid a time for it."

"We'll do no such thing!" My Mam went mad at him then. "You robbing bastard! I wonder that God don't strike you down dead, you wicked sod!"

"Ohhh, Effie . . ."

"Don't you bloody well 'Oh Effie' me! I knew you was low, Sidney Tompkin, but I never knew just what a snake you really are!"

"Ohhh, Effie!"

She rushed outside then and told the people, "Don't you dare leave any money here. Put it back in your pockets." And she picked it up and give it all back to them. Then chased them up the entry. When she come back she was all red in the face and really mad.

"Get in that house, Virgy!" She screeched. "And get off to bed! And no arguing back about it either. I've had enough of your bloody nonsense for one day. And you get to bed as well, Specs!"

It arn't fair, is it! Why should I get sent to bed when I've never done nothing? It wasn't me who saw the

Virgin Mary standing on our old mangle, was it? It arn't fair!

But I still had to go to bed.

Chapter Twenty-One

Uncle Harold loves his new job. He says that it's ever so interesting and instructive. The bit he likes the best is when he has to walk in front of the funeral procession wearing his top hat and tailcoat. He says that he feels really important when he does that, especially when the people stands still when he goes past, and the men takes their hats off. But he says the he likes all the other bits as well, and he reckons it's ever such a healthy job because he's getting exercise in the fresh air by walking down to the cemetery and back nearly every day. He says that he's never felt fitter in his life.

Uncle Sid laughs all scornful-like when Uncle Harold says how fit he feels, and tells him, ever so sarcastic, "Perhaps you might even get fit enough to help the others lift the bloody coffin one day, Harold. Instead of just prancing about like a big pansy in that bloody daft hat and coat."

When Hilda heard Uncle Sid say that she went mad at him. "You're just jealous of my Harold, you am, Sidney Tompkin. You hates it because he's doing so well in his new profession. Smiling Sam told me only yesterday that my Harold was the best thing to happen to the undertaking world since sliced bread. Smiling Sam says that Harold's bursting with fresh ideas and enthusiasm. He reckons that Harold's put new life into the business."

"New life?" Uncle Sid shouted, like he couldn't believe his ears, "New life? It arn't new bloody life that the business needs. It's new bloody death!"

"If you don't stop arguing there'll be two new deaths in this house in a minute." My Mam told them both off. "I'm sick of listening to you going on about Harold's job."

I reckon that my Mam arn't very happy about what Uncle Harold's doing, because I heard her telling Mrs Masters, "Our Harold's going over the top with this bloody funeral job, Florrie. He went and bought a roll of blackout the other day, and he's made a big black cloak out of it, that he can wear to the funerals. He's wrapped pieces of it round his tophat, and they hangs down in tails behind him, blowing in the bloody wind. He's asked Smiling Sam if it will be all right for him to carry a big black banner as well. He's made that already, the pole it's stuck on is as tall as a telegraph pole. You can see the bloody thing coming along over the tops of the bloody houses."

Mrs Masters roared with laughing and she told my Mam, "I shouldn't worry too much Effie, not until Harold starts bringing his work home with him anyway. When you finds a couple of coffins with the Stiff 'Uns in them under your table, then it'll be time to worry."

My Mam looked all worried then and she told Mrs Masters, "That's just it, my duck. He begun by bringing a load of pictures of funerals and coffins and gravestones home with him. Then he brought a shroud home with him the other day, because he said he wanted to study the needlework that went into it. Next thing you know

126

he'll be bringing the bloody coffins home, and after that it'll be the bloody Stiff 'Uns."

"What's he done with the shroud now then?" Mrs Masters wanted to know.

My Mam laughed then. "Hilda's copped hold of it. She reckons it's too good a material to waste on a Stiff 'Un, so she's going to make a couple of blouses out on it."

"Yeh, they'll look really nice and tasteful won't they," Mrs Masters said. "Especially with RIP embroidered on them in black."

My Mam roared with laughing. "Don't forget a nice wreath as well, Florrie, to add a bit of colour."

Just as my Mam said that, Mrs Masters stared and pointed down the street. "Is that your Harold coming, Effie?"

"Oh my God!" my Mam sort of groaned.

Uncle Harold was coming up the street wearing his top hat and tailcoat, and his new black cloak, and carrying his new black flag. And coming along behind him was Tommy TeeTee pushing a handcart, and on the handcart was a big coffin.

Tommy TeeTee was in his Salvation Army uniform, and wearing his wellies. He's not really in the Salvation Army, but they feels sorry for him and they gives him their old clothes to wear. Tommy TeeTee don't live in an house at all, he sleeps all over the place, under the hedges, in old sheds, anywhere he happens to be when he's drunk. That's why they calls him Tommy TeeTee, because he gets drunk six nights a week, and then every Sunday he goes to the Salvation Army Hall and swears he'll turn TeeTotal. Every Sunday night he sings in the Salvation Army Songster Brigade with all the women, and he plays the tambourine. He arn't half a good tambourine player as well, he whirls it round and round and the ribbons flies out like a catherine wheel. And when they'm all praying he keeps on standing up and shouting, "I was a wretched drunken sinner, and now I am saved! Hallelujah! Praise the Lord!"

And one of the Salvation Army men shouts, "Fire a Volley!" And they all stamps their feet and shouts "Hallelujah! Praise the Lord!"

Sometimes when the Salvation Army has a procession on Saturday nights, Tommy TeetTee runs out from the pub and tries to march along with them, but they don't let him when he's drunk, and they tells him to bugger off. Then he starts to cry and shout out, "Oh Sister Anna, let me help you to carry the banner!"

The woman who carries the Salvation Army banner in the procession arn't half tall and big, and Tommy TeeTee is ever so small, and when he shouts that at her she always gets hold of him by the scruff of his neck and shakes him, and she growls at him, "I'll 'Sister Anna carry the banner you', if you don't shurrup, you little toe rag!"

Anyway, Tommy TeeTee does odd jobs for Smiling Sam. Smiling Sam likes him a lot. He says that when Tommy TeeTee dies he's going to keep him in a mahogany display case. Smiling Sam reckons that Tommy TeeTee is so pickled in drink that he'll never ever rot away. He reckons that Tommy TeeTee will last for a thousand years in his display case. He says that Tommy TeeTee will be the first British Mummy.

When Uncle Harold and him got to our house with the handcart and coffin my Mam asked Uncle Harold, "What's you bringing that bloody thing here for?"

Uncle Harold looked all shocked, and told my Mam, "Come come, Effie, show a bit of charity. That's no way to describe Tommy is it! He's a human being, not a 'bloody thing'."

"I'm not talking about Tommy," my Mam told him. "I'm talking about that bloody coffin there."

Uncle Harold smiled all delighted-like, "Ahh, you've noticed it then, have you, Effie. Isn't it a beauty? Solid oak, every inch of it, and solid brass fitments, and look at this—" He opened the lid to show her. "This is a real satin lining with brass tacks. Fit for Royalty, this is."

My Mam give him one of her looks, "Don't keep wittering on, our Harold. Just answer my question, will you."

And he got a bit nervous then. "Well, Effie . . . well . . . well . . ."

"I told you before, our Harold. I don't want you bringing your work home with you. It's morbid. Real morbid. So you can take that bloody thing back to where you got it from."

She was ever so sharp, and Uncle Harold started to shuffle his feet and look down at the ground.

"Go on, take it back right this minute," my Mam said very firm.

"Well . . . well . . . I can't take it back, Effie." Uncle Harold was all red-faced and his lips was trembling like they always does when he's going to cry. I could see his glasses starting to steam up already.

"Why can't you take it back?" my Mam wanted to know. "If Tommy TeeTee was able to push it up the hill, I'm bloody sure he can manage to push it back down again."

"Well, Effie, I've bought it," Uncle Harold told her. "And Smiling Sam won't take it back now. He never takes back second-hand coffins."

"How can you call it second-hand?" my Mam shouted. "It ain't been used yet."

Uncle Harold was shuffling and looking all redfaced and tearful. "Well, it has been used sort of, Effie. I tried it out for size."

"Oh my God!" My Mam groaned and stared up at the sky, and lifted up both her arms and shouted, "Why? Why do you do this to me? I try to lead a good life, don't I? Just because I don't go to church don't mean to say that I arn't a Christian woman! Why do you do this to me?"

"I arn't done anything to you, Effie," Uncle Harold told her.

"Will you shurrup, our Harold!" she shouted at him. "I arn't asking you, am I?"

Then she shouted up into the sky again, "Why me? Why me?"

Mrs Masters was roaring with laughing, and Tommy TeeTee was laughing as well, but Uncle Harold was looking worried to death and he kept on looking up at the sky, and then at my Mam, as if he couldn't believe his eyes.

"It's not coming into this house." My Mam was very firm.

"But where can I put it?" Uncle Harold wanted to know.

"I can tell you one bloody place, but I don't think you'd be able to manage a thing that size," my Mam said, and then all of a sudden she looked like she was going to laugh, and she asked Uncle Harold, "What made you buy it?"

"I'm thinking of the future, Effie. I'm planning ahead."

"Oh my God!" My Mam was grinning now, and Mrs Masters told her, "He's got a point there, Effie. It's bound to come in useful one day, arn't it. And the way prices are going up he might have got himself a real bargain there."

"Well, then, why don't you make him an offer for it?" my Mam asked her. "Then you can have the bargain."

"No bloody fear!" Mrs Masters said. "I arn't planning to go to me own funeral for a good many years yet. And when I does they can put me in a cardboard box for all I cares. I arn't going to be able to see it, am I!"

"Maybe not, but you're going to be the main attraction on that day, arn't you, Florrie." My Mam was giggling now. "And you'll want to look your best for it, won't you? Seeing as how you'll be the star of the show."

'I don't think that it's anything to joke about, Effie," Uncle Harold said all solemn and shocked. "Funerals are very serious matters."

"Yes, they are, Harold." My Mam couldn't hardly speak for laughing. "Especially for the bugger who's lying in the coffin."

Her and Mrs Masters just fell against each other then, and they laughed and laughed and laughed.

But I was thinking of how good it would be if my Mam let Uncle Harold have his coffin in our house. Me and Johnny Merry couldn't half have some good games with it, couldn't we? We could play ghosts, and Dracula, and

131

Frankenstein, and when we got fed up with them games we could pretend it was a canoe and play Red Indians in it, and Eskimos hunting the whales. We might even be able to play at pirates in it, but I reckon it might be a bit too small for a pirate galleon. But it could make a good pillbox for our Jerry and Jap fighting games.

Well it started to rain then and Uncle Harold said, "Oh Effie, it'll be ruined if it gets left outside. This rain will ruin it."

"Oh, and I suppose that shoving it down a bloody big hole is going to do it a power of good, is it?" My Mam was still laughing, and then she shook her head and told him, "Oh all right then, you can bring it in. But it's got to stay up in the attic. I arn't having it where I can see it. I don't want to be thinking of death all the time."

They loaded the coffin onto Tommy TeeTee's back and he started to carry it upstairs, and he made such a rattle, bumping and clumping with it that Granny Smith woke up and come out of the back bedroom to see what was going on. When she saw the coffin she got all snotty and shouted at us, "You can't wait to get rid of me, can you, you cruel buggers! Well you needn't bother bringing that thing for me to get into, because I arn't ready to go yet. I shan't be ready to go for a bloody good while either."

"It's not for you, Mam," My Mam told her. "It's for our Harold."

"Our Harold?" Granny Smith looked all mystified. "It's for our Harold? Nobody told me he was dead. When did that happen? Mind you, for all the use or ornament the bugger is he won't be any loss, will he. But you should have told me anyway." Then she thought for a bit, and asked us, "Who'll scratch me back now then?"

Uncle Harold was all hurt in his feelings then, and he shouted up the stairs at her, "That's all you thinks of me as, arn't it Mother? I'm just a back-scratcher to you, arn't I!"

He flounced outside then grumbling and muttering to himself. "I can't get any pleasure, can I? The first present I buys myself and everybody resents it. I was really thrilled with my new coffin, but you lot have managed to take away all the pleasure I had in it."

He went and locked himself in the lav then, and he wouldn't come out for ages.

But I run to find Johnny Merry to tell him what I've got in my attic, and he reckons that we'll have some really good games with it. All the kids are jealous of me now that I've got a coffin in my attic. Me and Johnny Merry are going to play Dracula in it tomorrow, but Johnny Merry says that to play it properly we've got to fill the coffin with dirt from Dracula's castle. But I told him that we can use some dirt from the cemetery instead, because we can't go to Dracula's castle while there's a war on, can we? So tomorrow me and Johnny Merry are taking buckets down to the cemetery to fetch the dirt back in. It'll be a really good game, won't it.

After I come back from Johnny Merry's I went up into the attic to have another look at Uncle Harold's coffin.

Uncle Harold couldn't make his mind up whether to have it laying flat, or standing up in the corner. I helped him to stand it up in the corner and then he started walking from side to side to see how it looked.

My Mam come upstairs to see what we was doing and Uncle Harold asked her, "What do you think, Effie. Is that the right position for it?"

133

My Mam never said anything. She only looked up at the ceiling shaking her head.

"Of course, having it stood up like this certainly creates a most pleasing effect, doesn't it?" Uncle Harold was really happy. "It makes a sort of focal point for the room. Just look at that wood graining. And the brasswork positively shimmers where the light catches it. It's a proper work of art, arn't it, Effie?"

"Yes, it's too good to be buried in arn't it," my Mam said all sarcastic. "The worms won't half make a mess of that graining."

Just then Hilda come back from down town and when she come upstairs she shrieked, "What the hell is that doing here?"

"It's an investment that Harold's made," my Mam told her. "He's planning for his future."

"It don't look as if he's expecting any future by the look of things," Hilda shouted.

Uncle Sid come back from work then, and he come upstairs to see what all the noise was about.

"Oh, my God, Effie! Your brother's finally gone completely bloody doolally!" Uncle Sid said looking all disgusted. "I knew this would happen. I knew that having a job would drive him stark raving bonkers."

Uncle Harold stared at him all scornful-like. "I wouldn't expect a Philistine like you to appreciate a work of art, Sidney Tompkin."

Uncle Sid got all fierce then. "If you keeps on calling me filthy names like that in front of the ladies here, you'll be needing to use that bloody coffin sooner than you expects to use it, Harold."

Hilda and my Mam both turned on Uncle Sid then.

"Don't you make threats against my Harold, Sidney Tompkin, or you'll be having me to deal with!" Hilda shouted, and my Mam told him, "Yes, and I'll be helping Hilda if you so much as lays a finger on our Harold."

Uncle Sid got all huffy and went away then, and after a bit my Mam and Hilda had to go out as well.

"It's no good, Specs, I just can't resist it. I'm going to have to try it on for size again," Uncle Harold told me, and we put the coffin flat on the floor and Uncle Harold layed down into it.

He was smiling and chuckling to himself.

"My God, Specs, I had the bargain of a lifetime when I bought this. This is so comfortable. It's a perfect fit. Do us a favour, will you Specs, get hold of the lid and lay it on top. I wants to see how much space I'll have when it's screwed down."

The lid was laying on the floor by the side of the coffin, and it wasn't half heavy. I was really tired by the time I managed to get it on the top of the coffin. Uncle Harold had to help to slide it right over him. I couldn't hardly hear him speaking because he sounded all muffled and far away.

I couldn't find any screws to fasten the lid down with, but there was some sort of catches, and when I moved them they sprung shut over the side of the lid.

"Specs? Specs? Gerron down here this minute!" my Mam was shouting, so I banged on top of the lid and told Uncle Harold, "I'll only be a minute, Uncle Harold. My Mam wants me."

He said something, but all it sounded like through the wood was "Umma umma umma ummaaa."

"Run down to Old Bent's, Specs, and give him this list for me groceries," my Mam told me.

There was a big queue when I got to Mr Bent's and I had to wait ever such a long time before I could give him the list. When I come out of the shop again I saw Johnny Merry and Fatty Polson and Barry Fraser and Letty Dobbs over the road.

"Where are you going?"

"Down town," they told me. "To collect fag packets. A lot of Yanks in lorries has just been through so there'll be stacks of packets."

All the kids are collecting fag packets this week, it's the latest craze. Yank fag packets are the best. Camels and Lucky Strikes and Marlboros and Victory Vee's. But they're no good if they're ripped or dirty. They have to be still in the cellophane coverings to be really good. I arn't got many good Yank packets, but I've got a lot of Players and Gold Flakes and Woodbines, and some Pashas and De Reskes as well, only they're English and they're not as good to have as the Yanks.

"I'm coming," I told them, and we all went down town.

Well it was a real swiz! All the kids from down town was there already, and Mad Jack and his best friend, Filthy Cyril, was collecting the fag packets as well. They had a big sack, and what they was doing was waiting until they could see any of the little kids with any good fag packets, and they was robbing them off them. Mad Jack is as dirty as Filthy Cyril, because he sometimes helps the coalmen down the coalyard to fill the bags with coal.

My Mam told me that Mad Jack was ever such a good diver once. He used to climb right up to the highest board in the Swimming Baths and he used to dive off it. Then one day he was showing off with a special sort of dive, and he hit his head on the bottom of the baths and when he come back up to the surface he was as daft as a Bob Owler, and he's been as daft as a Bob Owler ever since.

You know what a Bob Owler is don't you? It's what we calls them great big moths who keeps on flying into the light bulbs and candles and burning themselves up. You've got to be really daft to do that, haven't you?

Mad Jack still does his dives, though. Only they won't let him into the Swimming Baths now because he's so dirty. But the coalmen lets him pile up a big pile of empty coal sacks, and he climbs up onto the top of the coalyard wall and he dives down onto the pile of sacks. The coalmen gives him money to do it. My Mam says that they're cruel for doing that, but Uncle Sid says that they're good to give him the money, because the silly daft bugger would do it for nothing anyway if they told him to.

Anyway, when we got down town there wasn't hardly any fag packets left to find. Only a few dirty ripped ones. We thought that we might as well go home again. Then Mad Jack and Filthy Cyril chased one little kid and took his fag packets off him, and he run home crying, and his big brother come with a gang of big kids to get Mad Jack and Filthy Cyril.

The big kids chased Mad Jack and Filthy Cyril all round the town, and we all run after to watch them. It was ever so good, one man was shouting, "Three to One on Mad Jack, Five to One on Filthy Cyril, Five to Four the Field!"

And the people in the shops was clapping and cheering.

When the big kids copped them outside the Rag and Bone Yard, Filthy Cyril dropped the sack, and run into

137

the yard, but Mad Jack had one of his fits. He shrieked and jerked and frothed and rolled all over the road, and a lorry nearly run over him, and the lorry driver stopped and jumped out and chased after the big kids with a big spanner in his hand, and all the big kids got fritted then and run away.

"Come on!" Johnny Merry shouted to us. "Let's grab hold of the sack and run."

But before we could get it, Filthy Charlie and Filthy Daisy come rushing out of the Rag and Bone Yard with one of their prams, and they threw the sack of fag packets into the pram and run back into the yard, and we was all too fritted to follow them up there.

We was too fritted because everybody says that judging from the stink in the yard Filthy Charlie must have at least a dozen bodies buried under the rubbish. And we reckoned that he might bury us under the rubbish as well if we tried to snatch the sack of fag packets from him.

Then we thought that we'd go scrumping in the Hostel gardens, but when we got there Miss Mason and Rodney were walking arm in arm around the gardens.

We hid in the bushes, and Johnny Merry shouted, "Yoo-hoo Grace! Yoo-hoo Rodney! Have you had any good Doo's lately?"

Miss Mason went all red in the face and she shouted, "I'm going to call the police, you cheeky little blighters!"

She stormed off into the house, but Rodney come charging towards us and we run away, and we was all roaring with laughing because Johnny Merry kept on shouting, "Think of your heart, Rodney! Remember your heart! Don't wank for at least a week!"

Then we thought that we'd go and see if Mrs Gibbs

was shouting. But when we got there the house was all quiet and the curtains was drawn.

"What shall we do now then?" Barry Fraser wanted to know.

We went down to the railway lines and played at ambushing the trains until it got late. Then Fatty Polson said, "It's supper time. I'm going home."

So we all went home.

When I got home my Mam and Uncle Sid and Hilda and Virgy and Granny Smith was all having their supper.

When she saw me my Mam said, "Oh, there you are. You shouldn't keep on tormenting me like this, Specs. I really believed that you'd finally run away, and I was so happy. Now you've gone and ruined my happiness again."

Virgy stuck her tongue out at me and said, "And I was happy as well, Mam."

Virgy really meant it. The nasty cow! But I know that my Mam don't really mean it.

"Well, once our Harold gets in we'll have all the circus here," my Mam said. "Have you seen him anywhere on your travels, Specs?"

"No, Mam," I told her. "Can I have a piece of jam?"

After she give me my piece, she said, "I wonder where our Harold's got to. It arn't like him to miss his supper, is it?"

"No, it most certainly arn't," Uncle Sid said, all sarcastic. "Harold never ever misses a meal, does he. If he felt the same about work as he does about eating, this country would produce more goods than the rest of the world put together."

"Are you sure you arn't seen our Harold, Specs?" my Mam asked me again.

139

"Not for ages, Mam. He was having a lay down when I left him."

"Where was he having a lay down?" Hilda wanted to know.

"In his coffin," I told her. "He said it was lovely and comfortable, as well."

"Oh my God!" My Mam sort of groaned, and Uncle Sid said ever so nasty like, "He don't need to practise being dead. He don't move fast enough for anybody to think he's alive as it is."

"He was still there when I went out, Mam," I told her. "I put the lid on him and fastened it down."

"OH MY GOD!" my Mam screeched. "When I heard all that bumping I thought it was the Salvation Army drum. The poor bugger will have suffocated to death by now!"

"You wicked little sod!" Hilda screeched at me, and threw her piece of bread and jam at me. "You'se murdered my darling Harold, you wicked little bleeder!"

"I never done nothing, Mam!" I got really fritted then. "Honest I never. Uncle Harold made me put the lid on him! Honest he did!"

"Shurrup Hilda!" my Mam told her, "and don't talk so daft. Specs wouldn't suffocate our Harold on purpose, you silly cow."

Uncle Sid smiled all smug like, and put on his posh voice. "Might I suggest, ladies, that you go and check if the silly bugger is still inside his coffin, before you assume that he's dead. Not that he'll be any bloody loss to the world if he has departed from this mortal coil, I might add."

"I'll mortal coil you if you don't shurrup, you snotty,

snidey bleeder." Hilda was shouting and bawling, and the tears was running down her face.

Then she jumped up and went running upstairs screeching, "I'm coming, Harold! I'm coming, my own darling. I'm coming, I'm coming, I'm coming!"

Uncle Sid only laughed. "That'll be the first time for years she's been able to shout that and mean it."

"You dirty-minded bleeder!" My Mam went mad at him. "How can you even think of such things at a time like this?"

Then she got up and run upstairs as well.

"Where are them two going?" Granny Smith wanted to know, and she started to moan and grumble. "I ain't had me second cup of tea yet, our Effie. You ain't give me me second cup of tea yet. You'se got no consideration for me, our Effie. No consideration."

"It's no good you going on at Effie, you silly old bat," Uncle Sid told her. "She can't hear you, can she! She's up in the bloody attic, arn't she."

"Do you reckon Uncle Harold is really dead upstairs, Uncle Sid?" Virgy asked him, and she was looking all excited.

"I can only live in hope," Uncle Sid told her.

Our Virgy clapped her hands and looked ever so pleased. "I've been waiting for somebody to die so that I can save their soul from Purgatory. I'm going to ask Our Blessed Lady to take him straight to heaven, and not leave him in Purgatory."

Then she run out into the back yard and went and kneeled down in front of her shrine and started singing a hymn.

I heard Hilda screeching and wailing upstairs, and I

felt so fritted that I couldn't eat my jam piece, and then my Mam come back downstairs, and she was laughing so much she couldn't speak at first.

"He's still alive then, is he?" Uncle Sid looked ever so disappointed.

My Mam nodded, and I felt ever so glad, because I like my Uncle Harold.

Then my Mam managed to tell us, "He arn't best pleased though. He's reckons that the coffin lining is ruined now."

"I'm surprised he was able to breathe," Uncle Sid said. "I'd have thought that he'd have used up all the air."

My Mam only laughed again. "No, he wasn't in any danger of suffocating, Sidney. But he did nearly drown himself. That's what all the bumping and banging was about. The water level was rising up to his nose."

Uncle Sid roared with laughing then. But I couldn't see what he was laughing about. My Mam was just being daft, I reckon. Because how could anybody drown themselves upstairs in an attic, I should like to know?

Chapter Twenty-Two

When me and Johnny Merry take my Mam's coal bucket down the cemetery to collect our Dracula Earth, we shall go at midnight. It has to be collected at midnight because that's what they does in the Dracula pictures. The cemetery's ever so creepy. There's a lot of big trees there, and an old chapel and another sort of shed where they puts the dead bodies of people who arn't got any families to keep them in the house until they'm buried.

When Billy Grover's old grandad from the bottom of our street died his family kept him in the house for ages. My Mam says that they had to keep him for such a long time because they'd drunk the Burial Club money so they couldn't pay for a funeral. Billy Grover is in my class at school. He's ever so scruffy, and he's always getting into trouble, but I like him because he can pee higher than anybody else in our street. He's the champion at peeing high of the whole school.

Well, when his grandad died all the curtains was kept closed in Billy Grover's house, and Billy told us that his grandad was laying on the table in the front room with a sheet over him. He snuck me and Johnny Merry into his house to show us his grandad, but when we opened the front room door it smelled all bad, and it was all dark and spooky, and we was too fritted to go right into the room and lift the sheet up to have a look at Grandad Grover. Billy Grover was too fritted to go into the room as well, which shows what a big fibber he is, because before we went to his house he told me and Johnny Merry that he used to go and lift the sheet to look at his grandad all the time.

Johnny Merry says that in the night the dead people comes out of their graves and wanders around the cemetery. He says that he's seen them, and that they're all dressed in long white gowns, and some of them are only skeletons, and some of them are rotting flesh. I was going to go with him the last time that he went to watch the dead people walking, but I fell asleep and couldn't get up from my bed at midnight, when we was supposed to meet outside Johnny Merry's house. Because I didn't turn up Johnny Merry said that I was fritted to go, but I wasn't. Well, only a bit fritted anyway.

There's a little house in one corner of the cemetery where the gravedigger lives. He's ever so creepy as well. Everybody calls him Quasimodo because he looks just like the Hunchback of Notre Dame looked in the picture. I saw that picture, it was ever so good. I liked it best when the Hunchback was jumping on the big bells and making them ring.

After we saw the picture, me and Johnny Merry tried to sneak up into the church tower down town so that we could jump on the bells and make them ring, but the bellringers caught us and one of them clouted us with the end of the bellrope. It didn't half hurt. When I told my Mam what the bellringer had done, she told me, "It serves you bloody well right.

It's a pity he didn't use the rope to hang you both with."

Anyway, when we goes down to the cemetery we has to be careful that Quasimodo don't catch us. Because if he does catch kids playing about in the cemetery he puts them into a grave and buries them alive.

Johnny Merry says that he knows three kids that Quasimodo has done that to. And he's says that he knows which graves that the kids am buried in. He's going to show me them when we goes to get our Dracula Earth.

We was going to go and get it last night, but we went to the Wolf Cubs instead.

There's a lot of different packs of Wolf Cubs in the town. They've all got different numbers and different coloured neckerchiefs. There's a lot of different Scout Troops as well but only the big kids can join them, and me and Johnny Merry aren't old enough yet to join the Scouts, so we joined the Cubs instead. We joined the Fifth, St Athelstan pack, because it's got a red neckerchief. We likes the red colour, because the man on the wireless says that the Red Army is brave and tough, so we thought that we'd like to wear a red neckerchief.

The man who's in charge of the St Athelstan Scouts and Cubs is a parson, the Reverend Horace Brunt, only we have to call him Akela. He wears a Scout uniform only he don't look very good in it because he's ever so tall and skinny and his shorts are long and baggy, and his Scout hat is all droopy and floppy, and it comes right down over his ears. Uncle Sid says that Akela looks like summat the cat dragged in.

We have some good games at the Cubs though. We plays 'British Bulldogs', and 'Knights on Horseback', and football, and sometimes Akela takes us up to the woods and we plays 'Prisoners Keep'.

In some of the other Cub packs the boys learns how to do all sorts of things likes knots and splices, and flags and woodcraft, but we don't learn anything, because Akela don't know anything about those sort of things. We learned how to Dib Dib Dib and Dub Dub Dub though. We have to all get into a circle with Akela in the middle, and we have to crouch down and pretend that our fingers are wolf ears, and we have to say all together, "Dib Dib Dib, Dub Dub Dub . . . Arrr Kayyy Laaa."

And Akela learned us some songs that we have to sing to him as well:

Ging gang gooliegooliegoolie Watcha,
Ging gang goo, Ging gang goo.
Ging gang gooliegooliegoolie Watcha,
Ging gang goo, Ging gang goo.
Hailah, hailashailah,
Hailah, shailah, Hailah Ho!
Hailah hailashailah,
Hailah shailah, Hailah Ho!

It's a daft song, ain't it!

Then we sings another song, it's this one!

Walls Ices, Walls Ices,
Eldorado! Eldorado!
Stop me buy one!
Stop me buy one!
Can't, ain't got no money!

I don't think that Akela likes me and Johnny Merry very much though. I don't think he likes us because we're the only ones who haven't got proper Cub uniforms to wear. All the others have got caps and neckerchiefs and woggles, and green jerseys and black shorts, and grey socks with red tabs, but me and Johnny Merry haven't got anything. My Mam says that she can't afford to use her precious clothing coupons to get me something that I'll only wear once a week. And Johnny Merry's big sister Doreen says that if that bleedin' Nancy Boy of an Arrykela wants Johnny Merry to wear a bleedin' woggle, he can bleedin' well buy it for Johnny Merry his bleedin' self. Because she's got no bleedin' intentions of ever wasting her bleedin' hard-earned money on a bleedin' silly useless thing like a bleedin' woggle!

So every week when we goes to the Cubs Akela makes me and Johnny Merry stand in front of the rest and tells us, "The Fifth St Athelstan's Cub Pack is justly renowned throughout the Scouting world for its smart turnout, and you two are a blot on our escutcheon."

I don't know what that means, but he says it ever so scornful like, and he glares daggers at us.

Then if he's takes us anywhere, he makes me and Johnny Merry walk right behind the rest of the pack on the other side of the road, so that nobody will know that we're part of it. And one day he told me, "If you are ever asked which Cub Pack you belong to, tell the enquirer that you are in the Seventh, St Anthony's. They're Low Church, you see."

Akela has got pets as well. He makes them all Sixers and Senior Sixers, and tells them to boss me and Johnny

147

Merry about. He's got one very favorite pet whose the Senior Senior Sixer, and just guess who that is?

Yeh! That's right! It's Aubrey, the posh kid from the top of our street.

Aubrey's Mam is the 'Brown Owl' of the St Athelstan Brownies, and Aubrey's Dad is the Chief Scout of all the Scouts in the town.

Uncle Sid was looking out of our front window one day and he saw Mr Jones-Evans wearing his Scout uniform, and he shouted to my Mam, "Effie! Just come and take a look at this Woggle Wearing Wanker."

When my Mam come to look, Uncle Sid said all scornful, "Just look at him, will you! What sort of an example is that for the lads? He's nothing but a prat. He wrote to the paper the other week asking people to contribute to funds for a new Scout Hut, and he signed the letter, 'Idris of the Scouts'. I ask you, 'Idris of the Scouts'! What a bloody prat!"

"Oh, I don't know," my Mam said all silky and nice. "Somebody told me that you wrote to the paper once, and signed the letter 'Sidney of the Guides'."

Then she laughed and walked off while Uncle Sid ranted and raved. I wonder why he was so mad? I'll ask Johnny Merry about it tomorrow.

Chapter Twenty-Three

Hey, guess what? I'm a film star! Yeh, it's true. Honest it is!

Yesterday afternoon it was Saturday, and me and the gang had all been to the picture club in the morning. Then we come back home and had our dinners, and then we all come out to play again. We was having a game of football in the street and the sun was boiling down, and all of a sudden a car and a big van come up the street and stopped outside Aubrey, the posh kid's house, and some men got out. So we stopped playing and all run to see what the men wanted.

Then Aubrey's Mam and Dad come out to talk to the men, and Aubrey's Mam was wearing her big fur coat and Cossack hat. I was ever so close to her and I could see her face was all red and sweaty because it was so boiling hot. Aubrey's Dad was wearing his Home Guards uniform, and Aubrey come out then and he was wearing a uniform just like his Dad's as well. I wished I could have a uniform like that. It looked ever so good.

After a bit they all went into Aubrey's house, and one of the men stayed in the van.

"What's you doing here, Mister?" Fatty Polson asked him.

"None of your business." The man was ever so miserable.

"Is this your van, Mister?"

"Where do you live, Mister?"

"Have you come to see Aubrey's Mam and Dad, Mister?"

"Shall you be here for a long time, Mister?"

"What's you got in your van, Mister?"

Johnny Merry poked his head in the van door and looked into the back. "Gorrr! Look at that!"

"Gerrout of it, you little sod!"

"You touch me and I'll get my Dad onto you, Mister."

"Is that a film camera, Mister? That big thing in the back there?"

"Ohhh, take a picture of me, Mister!"

"And me, Mister."

"And me, and me."

"Will you lot all bugger off before I clip your bloody earholes for you!"

"Just you try it, Mister." Johnny Merry pretended to be a boxer, and started jumping around in the road, ducking and bobbing and waving his fists. "Come on then, Mister. Let's have a fight!"

The man come roaring out of the van, and we all run' for it. It was smashing fun, because he was too old and fat to catch us. Then he got back into the van, and we all run back again.

"Will you take our pictures, Mister?"

"Is this your van, Mister?"

"Where do you live, Mister?"

Then Johnny Merry made me laugh, because he shouted

150

to the man, "Is that your nose, Mister? Or are you eating a banana?"

"I'LL BLOODY WELL FLAY YOU!" The man come roaring out of the van again. And we all ran away again. It was smashing fun.

But after we'd done it a few more times the man wouldn't chase us any more. He just laid over on the van bonnet gasping and panting, and trying to swear at us.

"Children! Children! Would you all come here for a moment, please."

Mrs Jones-Evans come out of the house and she had a brown paper bag in her hand. She said, "Children, come here please."

She was smiling at us! She'd never done that before!

"Come here, children. I've got some sweeties for you."

She was holding out the big brown bag, and smiling, and I kept on remembering about Red Riding Hood, so I wouldn't go near her. Nor would any of the gang.

"Look, they're barley sugars." She took a sweet out of the bag and Johnny Merry went up to her then, and she smiled at him and give him the sweet, and he brought it back to show us.

We all had a lick of it, and it was a real one. So then we all run up to Mrs Jones-Evans and she give all of us a sweet each.

"Now children, how would you all like to be film stars?" she asked us.

Then she told us to go home and fetch our tin helmets and our gas masks and our guns and to bring them to the big lawn at the back of her house. So we all run home and got our things and run back again. Some of the kids hadn't got guns, so they brought their swords instead, and some of them hadn't got tin helmets, so they made cocked hats from newspaper and wore them instead.

We haven't got real guns and swords and helmets, they're pretend ones that we makes ourselves from sticks and tin cans, but Aubrey had a real sword. It was all long and shiny and he couldn't lift it up and swordfight with it because he's such a weed. Me and Johnny Merry asked him if we could have a go with it, but he said no. Aubrey's always like that, you know. He never lets any of the kids in our street have a go with any of his things. That's why none of us likes him because he's like that. He's horrible, really.

Anyway, when we went onto the lawn the men had got a big camera on legs on top of the rockery, and one man was on the lawn talking to Aubrey's Mam and Dad. They was all talking into a microphone, and the men with the camera was taking their pictures. I snuck up close to listen to what they was saying.

The Man: "Captain Idris and Captain Mrs Sybil Jones-Evans, will you tell the British people what this war has meant to you?"

Idris: Looking all stern and brave. "It has given me the chance to serve my King and country, and to make any sacrifice that may be necessary in order to achieve victory over the Huns, the Ities and the Japs."

The Man: "Mrs Sybil Jones-Evans, will you tell the British people what this war has meant to you?"

Sybil: Looking all girlish and shy. "It has given me the opportunity to devote my life to helping those poor unfortunates in this town who have not had the good fortune to be as rich, intelligent, cultured and talented as myself."

152

Her voice gets louder and she don't look all shy and girlish now. "While my husband, Captain Idris Jones-Evans, is defending with great gallantry our beloved country from Adolf Hitler, Hermann Goering, Joseph Goebbels and all the evil Nazis; Benito Mussolini, Count Ciano and all the evil Fascists; Emperor Hirohito and General Tojo and all the evil Japanese; the treacherous Marshal Petain and all the cowardly, treacherous French, I myself am ceaselessly toiling among the ignorant, the afflicted, the misguided poor, and am slowly but surely by my example instilling in them some vestiges of my own high ideals of service, patriotism and love of our Royal Family, our Government, our Church and our beloved country."

The Man: "Thank you very—"

Sybil: Looking all stern and brave. "Women of the British Empire. Hear my call! I am the wife of a British Warrior. The Mother of a young British Warrior. I am a woman. A British Woman. Made in the same mould as Queen Boadicea, Queen Elizabeth, Queen Victoria—"

The Man: "Thank you Mrs Jones-Ev—"

Sybil: Shouting. "I call upon the women of the British Empire to rally behind me. To follow me in our battle against our enemies. To join with me in making whatever sacrifices must be made in order to achieve final victory. Women of the British Empire, follow me, onwards, united, one heart, one soul, one purpose. Onwards we go to victory. Women of Britain, Women of the Empire, Follow me onwards to victory. Three Cheers for Our beloved King and Country. Hip Hip Hip Hurrah! Hip Hip Hip Hurrah! Hip Hip Hip Hurrah!"

Sybil begins to sing in a high squeaky voice

153

God save our gracious King,
God save our noble King,
God save our King . . .

The Man looks at the men with the camera and makes throat-cutting motions. Then says, "Thank you very much, Captain Idris Jones-Evans and Captain Mrs Sybil Jones-Evans. Well, Adolf Hitler, now you can see why you will never win this war . . . Cut!"

The Man was all sweaty and pale and he went and sat down on the rockery, and when he lit his fag his hands was trembling and shaking.

After a bit, one of the men by the camera come down onto the lawn and told us kids, "Now we're going to film you lot. I don't want to see any laughing or gaming about. If you're good, then Mrs Jones-Evans will give you some sweets. If you play about, then you won't get nothing."

He made us line up and march up and down the lawn like soldiers, and he told Aubrey, "When we film this, Master Aubrey, you'll be standing on that stool over there giving the orders to this lot. All you have to shout is 'Quick March', 'About Turn, Halt'. And I'll give you the signal when to shout them."

"I'm not going to let Aubrey Snotface order me," Letty Dobbs said. "My Dad's a commando, and his Dad's only a Home Guard. It should be me standing on the stool ordering."

"You do what I say, or you bugger off," the man told her.

"I'll get my Dad onto you when he comes home again," Letty Dobbs told him, and said to me, "I'm going, Specs. Are you coming?"

154

I wanted to be on Letty's side, but I kept thinking about them sweets we was going to get from Aubrey's Mam. So I didn't know what to do.

Johnny Merry told me, "Stay here, Specs," and then he went to Letty Dobbs and whispered in her ear. And after a bit Letty grinned and she nodded. Johnny Merry come and whispered to me then. And after a bit I grinned and nodded, and me and Johnny Merry whispered to all the other kids, and they all nodded.

The man was getting a bit mad, I think, because he looked all daggers at us and he shouted, "What's it to be then? Make your minds up, I haven't got all day to waste."

"All right," we told him, and we all lined up.

Aubrey got on the stool at the end of the lawn, but then he fell off it, because his sword pulled him down on one side and he lost his balance and we all laughed.

The man was really mad now. "Get that bloody sword off him, somebody. And let's get on with it, shall we!"

The man with the microphone was feeling a bit better now, so he come and stood in front of the camera and said into the microphone, "Master Aubrey Jones-Evans is a worthy son of his Warrior father, Captain Idris Jones-Evans. While other boys of his age play games and waste their time in other ways, young Master Aubrey is doing his bit for the war effort. This remarkable, gallant young gentleman has raised his own regiment, and is training them to be ready for the time when they must join in the battle against Adolf Hitler and his evil henchmen. From what I've seen of Master Aubrey, or Colonel Aubrey as his loyal and adoring regiment admiringly calls him, then those Huns had better watch out when this gallant young

155

gentleman leads his soldiers into battle against them. You can take it from me that these soldiers are straining at the leash to follow their beloved young colonel into action. It'll be a case of, 'Watch out Adolf, you had better surrender, because here comes Colonel Aubrey to punch you on your nose.'"

The other man signalled then, and Aubrey started to shout orders and we all marched up and down the lawn. Some of the kids kept laughing, and messing about, and the men made us do it over and over again. After a bit Johnny Merry told us, "Get ready."

"Quick March!" Aubrey shouted.

"Charge!" Johnny Merry shouted.

And we all shouted "Charrggge!" and we run at Aubrey waving our guns and swords.

"Kill Colonel Aubrey!" Johnny Merry shouted.

"Kill Colonel Aubrey!" we all shouted, and Aubrey squealed and fell off the stool, and we all run right over him, and he was crying and kicking and shrieking.

"You little bastards!" Aubrey's Mam screeched and she come roaring after us, and she picked up Aubrey's sword and was trying to cut us to pieces with it. But we was all dodging and running, and laughing and shouting and she couldn't hit any of us. Then we all run out of her garden and got away. It was smashing fun. I should like to be a film star again, you know.

Chapter Twenty-Four

The Gyppoes have come to camp on the Old Rec down by the railway tunnel again, and all the grown ups in our street and the other streets are moaning about them. The grown ups don't like the Gyppoes, you see. They reckons that the Gyppoes pinches things from the gardens and the washing lines, and Granny Smith told me that the Gyppoes pinches Christian children as well, and takes them away with them in their caravans.

I told Johnny Merry what my Granny Smith had told me, and now he keeps on hanging about the Gyppoes' caravans, because he wants them to pinch him and take him away with them. Johnny Merry says that he wants to be a Gyppo because the Gyppo kids don't have to go to school, and don't have to wash their necks and behind their ears every day like we does. And the Gyppo kids don't get a tanning for going scrumping, or for getting muddied up, or for tearing their clothes like we gets a tanning for.

I reckon I should like to be a Gyppo as well, but only if my Mam come with me.

When Uncle Sid is at home my Mam always carries on about the Gyppoes, and she always tells me to keep away from them. She says that if she catches me hanging around the Gyppoes she'll tan the skin off my backside. But it arn't fair for her to tell me to keep away from the Gyppoes, is it. Because she don't keep away from them herself, does she. Because yesterday morning when Uncle Sid was at work, a Gyppo man come to our door selling pegs, and my Mam bought some off him, and stood at the door for hours talking and laughing with him.

When Hilda come home me and Johnny Merry come to get a drink of water in our back kitchen and we could hear my Mam telling her about the Gyppo man.

"He looked just like Tyrone Power," my Mam said, and she went "Gorrr! I couldn't half do summat for him, I'll tell you, Hilda. He had black curly hair and his teeth was ever so white, and he was built like Tarzan. Gorrrr! He was a real bit of all right, I'll tell you. I could have ate him!"

Then she pushed the kitchen door open and said to us, "What does you want, Big Ears?"

And Johnny Merry said ever so quick, "I'll have a piece of that Gyppo and three pennorth of chips please, Missus."

My Mam went all red and she didn't half catch Johnny Merry a clout on the earhole. While he was squawking and rubbing his earhole Hilda asked my Mam, "What did he say, Effie?"

"He said he'd have a piece of the Gyppo and three pennorth of chips," my Mam told her, and I could see that she was trying not to laugh.

But then Hilda said, "Never mind the bloody chips. Just give me a piece of the Gyppo, and you knows the bit I wants, don't you!"

And my Mam started laughing, and she give me and

Johnny Merry a drink of pop each and then told us to bugger off and leave her in peace. So we did.

We went down to the Old Rec to look at the Gyppoes. We had to sneak down there in case my Mam saw me, because she always says that I'm never ever to go near the Gyppoes' camp. When I was little I used to be fritted to go to the Gyppoes' camp because they all looks so tough, and there's always a lot of big dogs who comes to bark at us, but now I'm big I like going to look at them. But you've got to be careful of the Gyppo kids. Sometimes they're all friendly, and sometimes they tries to get us. But last time the Gyppoes come, me and Johnny Merry had a fight with the Gyppo kids, and we made one of their noses bleed, and made another cry, and after that they was friends with us, because they reckon that we're good fighters.

When we got to the Old Rec the Gyppoes was sitting round their campfires and one of the men called to us to come to him.

"Hello Chaveys," he said.

"Hello Mister Gyppo," Johnny Merry told him.

"What do you want here?" the man asked us.

"We wants to be Gyppoes, Mister," Johnny Merry told him.

The man said something in a funny language to the other men and women round the fire and they all laughed. Then he shook his head at us.

"That arn't possible, Chaveys. You've got to be born a Romany to be a Romany. Mind you, you could always become a Didikai, or a Tinker, I suppose."

"Can we come and live in your caravans when we're one of them?" Johnny Merry asked him, and the man shook his head again.

159

"No, my Chavey, we don't have such-like travelling with us. Only the Rom can travel with the Rom."

We was ever so disappointed, and I reckon the Gyppo felt sorry for us, because he said, "I'll tell you what though, my Chaveys. You can have a bit of grub with us now, if you likes to."

"Gorrr, yehhh," we told him. "Thanks Mister Gyppo."

There was an old woman there who looked just like a witch. She had long hair dangling down her face, and she was all shrivelled and wrinkled and brown, and she had all ragged clothes on and a turban wrapped round her head, and a big, hooked nose, and a pointy curled-up chin with whiskers on it.

There was a big old iron pot on the fire and it was full of stuff that was bubbling and smoking, and she kept on throwing stuff into the pot and stirring it with a long stick, and talking to herself.

I was a bit fritted of her, so I kept Johnny Merry between her and me. But Johnny Merry weren't fritted at all of her, and he asked the man, "Is she a real witch, Mister?"

"Why do you ask me that, Chavey?" the man looked a bit stern then.

"Well," Johnny Merry told him, "I've read about witches, and I've seen pictures of them and she looks just like the one in the picture I saw. Only she's uglier I reckon."

The man said something in a funny language to the other people, and they all stared at Johnny Merry ever so strange, and then at the old witch, and the man said something to her as well, and she looked daggers at Johnny Merry and hissed at him like she was a snake,

160

and he looked a little bit fritted. I was a lot fritted though. I was really fritted. Especially when she pointed her stick at us then waved it in the air and started to chant something in a funny language.

Then the man told me and Johnny Merry, "I'm sorry about this, my Chaveys, but my old woman is a real witch, and you've made her real angry. So she's putting a spell on both of you right this very minute. By tomorrow morning you'll be hopping around this town, because she's turning you both into frogs!"

We didn't half run away fast. And all the time we was running we could hear the people shouting and laughing, and the old witch screeching her spell.

When we got back to our own street we was out of breath, and I had a big stitch in my side and it wasn't half hurting me.

"What shall we do?" I wanted to know.

But Johnny Merry was too fritted to tell me anything, so we both run home.

I told my Mam that the old witch had put a spell on me, and that I should be turned into a frog by tomorrow morning.

"What?" she shouted, and she made me tell her everything that had happened.

"What shall we do, Mam?" I was nearly crying. Well, really, I was crying I suppose, because my eyes was all wet and my throat was all chokey.

"I'll have to think about this for a minute or two, Specs." She was looking all solemn.

Then, all of a sudden, she looked at me and pointed her finger into the air. "I've just thought of something, Specs. I've got the answer to this problem all right. I'll

161

get the bath out of the coal shed and put it in the back yard and fill it with water, and you can live in it. All the other frogs will be dead jealous of you when they see your new pond. They'll think that you're Royalty."

"Ohhh Mammm, I don't want to be a frog. I want to be a boyyyy!" I was really crying now. "I don't want to be a frog. I want to be a boyyyyy!"

"Oh, you want to be a boy, do you? You disobedient little sod!" She went mad at me then. "What have I told you about not going near them bloody Gyppoes? What have I told you? Well I'll show you another bloody spell, and believe me when you've seen my spell you'll wish you had changed into a bloody frog. I'll change you back into a boy all right, believe me!"

She grabbed hold of me and slung me over her knees and give me such a tanning. And while she was giving me a tanning she kept on shouting, "This is the strongest bloody spell in the world! Stronger than any bloody Gyppo can put on you!"

When she'd finished I asked her, "Will I still change into a frog now, Mam?"

"No, you bloody well won't change into a frog, you silly little bugger. Worse luck for me! Now get to bed before I give you another bloody tanning, and keep away from those soddin' Gyppoes."

My backside was ever so sore. But I didn't care, because I knew that I wasn't going to turn into a frog now. My Mam's spells are stronger than any other witches' spells in the whole world, you know.

Hey, I've just thought of something. How about Johnny Merry? If nobody gives him a tanning he'll turn into a frog tonight, won't he.

162

I'll ask my Mam if he can come and live in the bath in our backyard, then I can look after him then, can't I? And stop the other frogs from picking on him.

Chapter Twenty-Five

Mr Splies who lives at the bottom of our street is all crooked. He's all twisted and bent over so that his head is nearly on the floor, and when he walks he can't hardly see in front of him. Johnny Merry calls him the 'Hairpin Bend'.

My Mam says it's cruel to mock the afflicted, and nobody can blame Mr Splies for being such a miserable sour bastard. She says that his affliction would turn anybody sour. But then when she saw him coming up the street one day I heard her tell Uncle Sid, "Just come and look at Splies, will you, Sid. They ought to call him, 'Here's me head, me arse is coming'." And they both laughed.

Well, what I wants to know is, why does she tell me off for calling Old Splies the 'Hairpin Bend', and then go and call him, 'Here's me head, me arse is coming' herself? That's cruel, aren't it.

Anyway, all the grown-ups says that Mrs Splies is a martyr and a saint to put up with Old Splies, because they says that he's the Devil Incarnate to live with. They says that he hits her with a big stick that he keeps by the side of his chair, and I heard my Mam telling Hilda that when Old Splies is on the drink he makes Mrs Splies take off

all her clothes and do things to him. I don't know what
things they are, because when my Mam saw me listening
she shut up and told Hilda, "I'll tell you later, my duck,
when Noddy Big Ears aren't around."

I asked Johnny Merry what sort of things Old Splies
made Mrs Splies do to him when she hadn't got any
clothes on. Johnny Merry knows all about things that
women does when they haven't got their clothes on,
because he always spies on his big sister, Doreen, when
she takes her clothes off. You know Doreen's boyfriend
was a Blackie from America, well he isn't any more.
He's a Pole. Doreen says that he's a Count. Just like
in that film, "The Count of Monte Cristo". Doreen and
my Mam are friends again now, and when my Mam met
Doreen and her boyfriend in the street, Doreen's boyfriend
bowed to her and clicked his heels together just like the
Jerries does in the pictures. My Mam said it made her feel
like a right prat because some boys saw him do it, and
they followed her up the road bowing and clicking their
heels together, and shouting, "Heil Hitler! Ve haff ways
off making you talk!"

Well, Johnny Merry told me that when Old Splies
makes Mrs Splies take her clothes off, then he makes
her dance on the table. She has to do the Belly Dance,
and the Dance of the Seven Veils. I read in a book about
the Dance of the Seven Veils. It said in the book that the
women who does it gets given a man's head that's been
chopped off and put on a plate. Johnny Merry says that
he knows a woman who's called Salome, and she does
the Dance of the Seven Veils in one of the pubs down
town. Johnny Merry says that all the Yanks goes to see
her do the dance, and when she does it they gives her a

166

man's head on a big silver plate. He says that they gets the heads from Smiling Sam and KKKK Katie KKKKoffin.

I asked Uncle Harold about that, because Uncle Harold works for Smiling Sam and does all the funerals for him. When I asked him, Uncle Harold looked all thoughtful. He had a row last week with Quasimodo the grave digger down at the cemetery, because Uncle Harold says that Quasimodo pinched his black banner and buried it with one of the Stiff Uns, and now Uncle Harold hates Quasimodo. Uncle Harold says that Quasimodo's real name is William Burke and that his missus is really a man named William Hare, only he's wears a disguise that makes people think that he's Mrs Quasimodo. Uncle Harold says that Burke and Hare used to pinch dead bodies and sell them to the doctors to cut up and play about with. So when I asked him about the heads that the Yanks gives to Salome in the pub down town he looked all thoughtful and then he told me, "You've given me food for thought, Specs." And he nodded all wisely. "Yes indeed, you have given me food for thought."

But then he just wandered off, and never said anything else about it, and when I asked him again the next day about it, he just said, "I'm still digesting the food for thought that you gave me yesterday, Specs." And he wandered off again, humming to himself.

Uncle Harold hasn't got his coffin now, you know. My Mam chopped it up for firewood. I got a tanning for it, because they all said that it was my fault it had to be chopped up. Well it wasn't me to blame. It was Johnny Merry's fault.

Hilda said that the sight of the coffin standing in the corner of the attic give her the willies, and so she made

167

Uncle Harold keep it under their bed so that she couldn't see it when she went upstairs to the attic. When my Mam and Uncle Sid and all the rest was at work and there was only Granny Smith in the house, me and Johnny Merry used to go up to the attic and pull the coffin out from under the bed and play games in it. It used to smell a bit, because of what Uncle Harold did when he was locked in it that time, but we had some smashing games. We used to play explorers and pretend it was our boat, and we used to play submarines and pull the lid down over us when we submerged. And then we played "Bombers" and made it into a Lancaster bomber over Germany, but Granny Smith used to try to spoil that game because when we dropped our bombs she used to shout up the stairs and tell us, "Just you wait 'til your Mam gets home, you little bugger, and I tell her about you chucking bricks out of the attic window. She'll tan the backside off you."

We didn't take any notice of Granny Smith because she's still having one of her funny turns, so my Mam wouldn't believe her when she told her about us. But then Mrs Berrod from West Street told my Mam that we was shouting "Bombs Away!" and dropping bricks on her every time she walked under our attic window. So we had to stop playing that game. And I got a tanning for it as well. But Johnny Merry never got a tanning for it, did he!

One of the best games we played was Dracula. We used to frit the other kids to death with that game. It was smashing! We borrowed Uncle Sid's spare set of false teeth and we filed them into two long fangs like Dracula's got, and we got some lipstick and face powder from Doreen's handbag, and some soot from the chimney,

168

and we found a bed sheet hanging on a line at the back of Aubrey, the posh kid's house. Then me and Johnny Merry used to take turns as dressing up like Dracula, with all red lipstick round our mouths like blood from our victims, and black soot around our eyes, and powder on our faces to make us look like we was the 'Living Dead'. Then the one whose turn it was to be Dracula used to wrap the sheet round us and lie down in the coffin, and put Uncle Sid's fangs into our mouth. They looked ever so good. Just like the real Dracula's fangs. Then one of us would go down and ask any of the kids if they wanted to come up to the attic and play. Oh, I forgot to tell you before. We used to draw the curtains in the attic so it was all dark and creepy. When the kid come up to play, we used to say, "The toys are in that big box. Can you get them out for me."

Some of the kids used to say, "It's a coffin, aren't it?"

And we use to tell them, "Yeah, but nobody uses it, so we keeps our toys in there now."

And the kids used to open the coffin lid, and Dracula would hiss ever so loud and jump up at them.

The kids would scream out and go roaring down the stairs, and me and Johnny Merry would kill ourselves laughing.

All the kids liked that game, you know. And some of them kept asking us to let them come up to the attic and open the coffin lid even after they'd done it before. And it always used to frit them, even when they knew that it was only me or Johnny Merry pretending to be Dracula.

Then one day we was playing and it was my turn to be Dracula, only when Johnny Merry went down to find a kid to bring upstairs, Uncle Sid come home early from

169

work. And he come up to the attic, and I thought it was the kid coming up with Johnny Merry, and I kept ever so quiet and waited for the lid to open, and when it did I hissed ever so loud and jumped up. Uncle Sid fainted and fell down, and I thought he was dead, and I run away and I hid on the railway bank in the bushes. It was Hilda who found me, and she was laughing about Uncle Sid fainting, and she kept on saying, "Just let him try to give me any more bullshit about night fighting in the jungle again."

But when we got home my Mam was ever so mad and she kept on screeching at me, "You could have give poor Sidney a bloody heart attack, you wicked little sod."

And she give me a tanning, and then she dragged the coffin down to the yard and chopped it up for firewood.

Uncle Harold was all tearful, and he kept on begging her, "Not that, Effie. Not that. It's not the coffin's fault, is it?"

She just shook the axe at him and give him one of her looks, and he went all white and never said another word.

Uncle Sid was laying in bed, drinking a bottle of brandy that my Mam bought him to help him get better again, and Hilda just clucked her tongue and said, "Trust that bleeder to fall on his feet."

But my Mam told her, "That shock would have killed a weaker man, Hilda. I just thank the Lord that Sidney is such a tough nut."

"Bloody monkey nut, you mean," Hilda told her.

That was a good joke to say, wasn't it? Uncle Sid is a Monkey Nut. Hahahahaha!

*   *   *

Anyway, Old Splies did it again this afternoon. He went to the pub at dinner-time and told everybody that he was going to do it. And then he went back home and did it. He put his head in the gas oven, and he turned on the gas.

Lots of people does that round our way. They lays down on the floor, and they puts a cushion or a pillow inside the gas oven to put their heads on, and then they turns on the gas. A lot of the women keeps on saying that they're going to do it, but some of them don't. Some of them do though. Mrs Cartwright at the top of our street had a big row with her husband, Mr Cartwright, and all us kids was playing outside and we could hear her shouting, "I'm going to put my bloody head in the gas oven. I can't stand any more of this. I'm going to end it all. I'm going to stick my head in the gas oven."

And then Mr Cartwright come to the door and he stood on the step and when a man went past he asked him, "Hey mate, have you got any silver you can give me for this ten bob note?"

The man sorted out all his change and give it to Mr Cartwright, and Mr Cartwright give him the ten bob note. And then the man asked him, "What does you need all that change for?"

"My missus is going to stick her head in the gas oven, and I wants to make sure that the meter's full so that the gas won't run out."

They both roared with laughing, and while they was laughing Mrs Cartwright run out to the door and she hit Mr Cartwright over his head with a chopper and he fell down and the blood was running out from his head all across the step and the other man run to fetch a policeman.

Mrs Cartwright went into my house to have a cup of

171

tea with my Mam while she was waiting for the policeman to fetch her, and my Mam wouldn't let me come into the house, so me and Johnny Merry snuck up to the window and listened to what they was saying.

Mrs Cartwright was all joyful and she kept on telling my Mam, "That give the bugger a shock, didn't it! He wasn't expecting that, was he! That give the bugger a shock, didn't it! He wasn't expecting that, was he." Then she said, "Bloody shame about the step though. I only cleaned it this morning and it's all messed up now."

The ambulance come and took Mr Cartwright to the hospital to have his head mended. And does you know summat, Mr and Mrs Cartwright was walking arm in arm down our street the very next day, and he had a big bandage wrapped round his head, and she was wearing a new pinafore.

This afternoon, when Old Splies did it again, my Mam told Hilda that Mrs Peters from across the road run into the shop where Mrs Splies works, and told her, "Your old man is doing himself in."

Mrs Splies said, "Oh yeah? How's he doing it?"

"He's sticking his head in the gas oven," Mrs Peters said. "You'd better run home fast if you wants to stop him."

"Phooo!" Mrs Splies just looked all disgusted and shook her head. "There's no need for me to run home. He can't get his head in the oven, not the way he's shaped. His feet gets in the way."

My Mam didn't half laugh when she told Hilda this, and then said. "It's true, Hilda. The old sod can't get his head into the oven because he can't straighten himself up enough to do it. His feet bangs against the gas stove and stops him. If I was his missus I'd buy him a gas poker. He could put that between his legs and get his head right over it."

Mrs Peters says that she going to complain to the landlord about having to live opposite Old Splies. She says that if he keeps on filling the house with gas, one of these days somebody is going to come by and strike a match to light his fag and then the whole street will be blown to Kingdom Come. She says that Old Splies is a bigger danger to this street than the whole of the Jerry Airforce put together, because he's more likely to blow us all up than they am.

Chapter Twenty-Six

I saw a ghost last night! Yeah, really! I saw a real ghost.
We all saw it. There was me and Johnny Merry and Fatty
Polson and Terry Murtagh. We was all playing round the
old lamp post at the top of our street when we saw a ghost.
Now that the dark nights has come again we always likes
to play round the lamp post. None of the lamp posts in our
street was ever lit, and then this year when the dark nights
started some men come up our street and fixed a sort of
black shade around the light and now the lamp lights up
for a bit every night. But because of the black shade there's
only a circle of light just underneath the lamp and it don't
spread out at all.

Uncle Harold said that the lamps being lit was like a poetic
oasis in the Sahara Desert. He said that they was beacons
of hope and comfort to the weary traveller, and to the
sailor coming home from the sea and the hunter coming
home from the hill and the soldier coming home from
the war.

Uncle Sid laughed all scornful. "You'm forgetting the
most important one, Harold. The Piss Artist coming home
from the pub."

"That's just typical of you, aren't it, Sidney Tompkins!"
Hilda went for him then. "You soils everything with your
filthy mind."

"What?" Uncle Sid stared at her and his eyes was all
bulgy like he was amazed. "What have I said that's
filthy?"

Then my Mam joined in. "You'm just lowlife, you am,
Sid Tompkins. Our Harold's just said a beautiful thing,
and all you can do is to come out with your filthy talk."

Uncle Sid looked all hurt then, and he got up from the
table and told them, "I wish that I'd stayed in the Foreign
Legion, because living here with you lot is like living with
a bunch of bloody mad Touregs anyway. At least in the
Foreign Legion I had comrades to share the suffering and
death with."

"The nearest you've ever been to the bloody Foreign
Legion is watching 'Beau bloody Geste' at the pictures,
and then you had to come out before the picture finished
because you couldn't stand the sight of blood!" my Mam
told him.

Uncle Sid looked all noble and proud then, and he told
her, "I had to come out before the picture was finished,
because it brought back too many awful memories. Too
awful to be endured. I saw my *bong camarades* dying
again before my very eyes. I saw Beau and John and
Digby fighting and dying for La Belle France, just like
me and my *bong camarades* did in the desert sands."

"Well, you and your comrades didn't do much fighting
and dying when the bloody Jerries invaded La Belle
bloody France, did you," Hilda screeched. "That's why
we had Dunkirk."

Uncle Sid looked at her as if he'd been cut to the

quick and he said all tragic like, "You talk to me about Dunkirk. By God, I could tell you summat about Dunkirk! By God, I could tell you summat about it. By God, I could. By God!"

"Come on then, tell us summat about Dunkirk." Hilda was grinning like the cat that's got the cream. "Come on, we're all listening."

Uncle Sid frowned all stern at her. "You knows very well that my lips are sealed. I gave my solemn word, my sacred oath, to somebody very high-up, that I would not tell about my heroic deeds, or tell the truth about what really happened at Dunkirk, until that very high-up person gave me permission to speak out."

"And who is this very high-up person, might I ask?" Hilda was all triumphant then. "Let's hear his name."

My Mam laughed and told her, "It's Arthur Coxall the window cleaner. He's really high-up, aren't he. All of six feet up the ladder when he cleans the Gas Office windows."

Uncle Sid got mad then, and he shouted at them, "That's it. I'm leaving! And you'll be sorry when I've gone."

My Mam and Hilda looked at each other, and they was grinning all over their faces, and then they started singing ever so loud:

> *I'll join the Legion, that's what I'll do,*
> *And in some far distant region*
> *I shall start my life anew . . .*

Then they bust out laughing, and Uncle Sid walked out swearing and cussing.

I reckon they'm cruel to Uncle Sid sometimes. Because I saw that film, 'Beau Geste', and them Touregs am ever so fierce. Uncle Sid must have been brave to fight them, mustn't he? I mean, them Touregs killed every one of the Foreign Legion in Fort Zinderneuf, didn't they? I shall ask Uncle Sid to tell me about when he was in the Foreign Legion. I wonder if Uncle Sid ever met Beau Geste and his brothers? Anyway, we all saw a ghost last night. Yeah, it's true, we really did see one.

You see, when it's the dark nights our gang plays some good games. Like 'Devil up the Drainpipe', and 'Tapper at the Window'. They don't half make people fritted when we plays them. For 'Devil up the Drainpipe' we gets some newspapers, or better still some paraffin rags, and we creeps up in the dark to where there's a house with a drainpipe running down by the living room window. We stuffs the rags and paper up the drainpipe and then we sets fire to them. The flames goes roaring up the pipe and makes ever such a loud howling sound, just like there's a werewolf outside. All the people in the house comes running out bawling and shrieking, and shouting that they'll kill us when they catches us. But they can't see us in the dark, can they. Johnny Merry showed me that game, but it's a game that we can't ever tell anybody else about, because my Mam says that if she ever catches me playing 'Devil up the Drainpipe', then she'll have me put away in a home for wicked boys, where they feeds you on bread and water, and whips you every single day.

'Tapper at the Window' is good as well. What we does is to creep up to the window and we pushes a pin into the wood part. Then we fixes a piece of black cotton to the pin and dangles a button from it. We ties another long piece of cotton to the button, or to a pebble if we haven't got a button, and we hides in the dark and keeps

178

on tugging at the long piece of cotton. This makes the pebble rattle against the window glass. The people inside thinks that it's a ghost tapping the window and they don't half get fritted.

Johnny Merry used to play 'Tapper at the Window' with old Mrs Berrod down West Street, and he told me that she used to scream and shout for the neighbours to come and save her from the ghosts. But one night when he was fixing the button onto the window she leaned out of the upstairs window and dropped a housebrick on his head. He told me that he had to go to the hospital and have an operation because the brick broke his skull. He told me that the doctor told him that if it had been a blue brick that Mrs Berrod had dropped on him, instead of a red brick, then his head would have been smashed flat, because the blue bricks are a lot heavier than the red bricks. Johnny Merry said that the policeman asked him if he would like to get Mrs Berrod put in jail for trying to murder him, and Johnny Merry said, yes, he would. But Mrs Berrod promised Johnny Merry that if he'd let her off, then she'd give him all her money and her house when she died. And she said that she'd always be grateful to him and be his friend for life if he didn't make the policeman take her to jail, and that she was very sorry for what she'd done, and she'd never do anything like that again. So Johnny Merry let her off, and he says that me and him will live in her house when she dies, and have all her money to spend. That'll be good, won't it! But what I can't understand is that Mrs Berrod always shakes her fist at Johnny Merry when she sees him, and shouts that she'll bloody well flay him when she cops hold of him, and then she chucks stones at him.

Another thing that I can't understand is why Johnny Merry never had a bandage on his head when he had the operation? But when I asked him about that, he told me that the doctor had used a magic ointment which mended everything straight away, so he didn't have to have a bandage on his head. I bet we'll have some fun when we gets Mrs Berrod's house to live in though.

Well, last night we thought that we'd play a game on the Hostel girls. So what we did was to get a cardboard box and cut some holes in it so that it looked like an evil spirit's face. And we lit a candle and stuck it inside the box and crept up to the Hostel windows and put the evil spirit's face against the window. All the girls shouted and screamed, and we laughed and run away. Well, we did this a few times, but it wasn't so good then, because the girls just shouted at us, "Piss off, you bloody kids!"

See, they knew it was us, and not an evil spirit, so it wasn't any fun to do it again.

We went under the lamp at the top of the street, and we could hear Fatty Polson's Mam shouting for him to come in. And then my Mam started shouting for me to come in as well, and I shouted back that I was coming and she went back into our house and closed the door. I was just going to go home when from out of the Hostel gates this woman come walking. She was all black and when she got close we could see her face and it was all white. She had her arms out pointing towards us, and she was wearing a long, black dress and her hair was all long and hanging down. We thought it was one of the Hostel girls trying to scare us, and we all started laughing, and chucking stones at her. She just kept on coming towards us, and she never said a word and Johnny Merry shouted at her, "You can't frit us, you silly cow."

And she still never said anything, and her face was ever so white and funny and when she got to the light we saw that she hadn't got any eyes, and then she just disappeared. She just went, and there was nothing there.

We didn't half skreek and run then. We was all fritted to death! I run into my house and told my Mam that we'd just seen a ghost, and she just looked at me, and she never said anything for a bit. And Uncle Sid said, "The little bleeder's having you on, Effie."

But Hilda told him, "Just shurrup a minute, Sid. Look at the kid's face, will you. He's not having us on at all. He's as white as a sheet."

My Mam made me stand in front of her and tell her what we'd seen, over and over again, and she was looking ever so worried, and then there was a knocking on the door, and everybody jumped and shouted out like they was fritted as well.

It was Mrs Polson come to ask me about what we'd seen, because she said that Fatty Polson was in the house and he was crying and playing up something cruel because he reckoned that he'd seen a ghost.

Then Johnny Merry's big sister, Doreen, come to the door as well, and she brought Johnny Merry with her, and he was looking ever so fritted as well. All the grown-ups kept on asking us to tell them about what we'd seen, and after a bit they all believed us, because we was telling the truth.

My Mam thought for a bit, and then she said, "I'm going to go and see Esther Lee about this."

181

Uncle Sid told her, "Don't talk so sarft, Effie, what can that bloody old witch do about a bloody ghost?"

"She can tell us what it wants," my Mam told him. "She can talk to the dead, Esther can."

"That's all codswallop!" Uncle Sid don't believe in anything like that, you know. "That's just codswallop that she tells to silly buggers like you lot."

Well, all the women went for him when he said that. Hilda and Doreen Merry and my Mam and Mrs Polson all started shouting at him and calling him names, and telling him that he was the stupid silly bugger, not them.

Uncle Harold sat smiling ever so smug and saying, "That's right, girls. You tell him where he gets off. Give it him hot and strong!"

In the end, Uncle Sid jumped up and ran off out to the pub, and the women all cheered and clapped as if they'd won a match.

My Mam put her coat on and said that she was going to fetch Esther Lee to our house. I'm fritted of Esther Lee, you know. All the kids am. None of us ever dares to play tricks on her, or to give her any cheek. She's a proper witch. A real one, not a pretend one.

She looks like a Gyppo, and she's all brown and black and her eyes are ever so big and dark and shiny, and she has her hair done up in rings around her ears. She's not very big but she's ever so strong. When somebody dies in our street they sends for Esther Lee to come and lay the body out, and I heard my Mam telling Hilda that Esther Lee gets rid of babbies, as well. She's ever so cruel and bad to do that, aren't she? Because babbies are ever so tiny and weak, aren't they? They can't fight or run away, can they? But I don't know where she puts the babbies when she gets rid of them. We throws our dead goldfish down the lav. And when my Mam drowns the kittens we digs a hole down the garden and buries them there. But I don't know what Esther Lee does with the babbies. My Mam told Hilda that Esther Lee got rid of Doreen Merry's babby. She said that first of all Esther Lee tried hot baths and a bottle of gin. Then she made Doreen jump from the top to the bottom of the stairs. I thought, what daft things to do. What difference does it make to the babby if Esther Lee puts gin in her bath, or Doreen jumps downstairs or no?

My Mam told Hilda that when nothing happened, then Esther Lee used the knitting needle and that did the trick. Well, I was listening behind the door, and I didn't know what my Mam was going on about because Doreen Merry hasn't got a babby at all. She's never had a babby. So I thought that my Mam was getting mixed up, and so I come out from behind the door and I told her that she was all mixed up because Doreen Merry hadn't got a babby, so how could Esther Lee have got rid of it? Because you can't get rid of something that you haven't got, can you? But my Mam wasn't a bit pleased when I told her that she was all mixed up about Doreen Merry and a babby. She just went mad at me for hiding behind the door, and she give me a tanning for being a sneaky little bleeder.

Esther Lee tells fortunes as well, you know, I heard my Mam telling Hilda all about it one day. My Mam said that all the policemen's wives go to have their fortunes told by Esther Lee. My Mam said that the policemen's wives takes Esther Lee packets of butter, and tea and bacon and eggs and all the other stuff that's on the ration. They can give her lots of stuff because the policemen are like the rich people and the Royalty, they gets everything they wants from the Black Market. My Mam says that it's only the poor silly buggers like us who has to go short. She says that in this country them that works the hardest are the least provided for, and them that does the least gets the most. Hilda laughed then, and said, "Well, there's one thing that aren't on the ration, my duck, that we can get as much of as the rich buggers."

My Mam laughed as well and said. "I wish you'd tell Sid that. Because just lately you'd think it was on the ration judging from the little bit he gives me. I'm beginning to wonder if he's giving it to somebody else!"

I wondered what she was talking about it. Was it sweets or something? So I asked her what Uncle Sid was only giving her a little bit of? She told me to mind my own business, and she clouted me for being a nosey little bleeder. So then when Uncle Sid came home from work, I asked him about it, and he went all red in the face, and he just mumbled summat that I couldn't hear. So I asked him again, and he just told me to shurrup and mind my own business. Well, I reckon if he's giving his sweets to somebody else and not to us then it is my business, isn't it? I should like to know who he is giving his sweets to, I should.

When my Mam come back to our house with Esther Lee, Johny Merry run out of the door, and he wouldn't come back, and Doreen couldn't catch him to make him come back. I wanted to run away myself, but the grown-ups got hold of me and I couldn't get away. I was ever so fritted when Esther Lee pulled me close to her and stared at me with her dark shiny eyes. And then she said,

"I smell death here. I smell lilies, the sure omen of approaching death."

I started to cry, I was so fritted.

All the grown-ups was fritted as well, all their faces was ever so white.

"Stop crying, boy," Esther Lee told me, and because I was so fritted of her, I did.

"Now tell me, boy, what you saw. Describe that woman to me. I need to hear everything about her down to the smallest detail. I must know everything."

So I told Esther Lee everything about the ghost, and after I told her she nodded all wise and solemn.

"I know her," she said. "It's the maid who was killed by lightning in the Big House, when it was a private dwelling place many years ago. My grandmother laid her out. The only mark on her body was a star-shaped burn where the lightning had gone into her. She's getting lonely again and she's seeking a companion to join her on the other side."

"Oh my God!" My Mam put her fingers in front of her mouth like she does when she is really fritted of something.

Esther Lee nodded, all solemn. "It's happened before, several times in fact. The maid gets lonely and she comes to find a companion. Those who see her are in mortal danger, because she'll take one of them to dwell with her in the shadowy land beyond the grave. She's done it before. My grandmother, my mother, and me as well, have all laid out the bodies of the maid's victims."

"Oh, my God!" All the grown-ups was fritted to death now.

Esther Lee stroked my face, and said, all sad, "You poor boy. So young. So young. You poor boy!"

"Ohhh noooo!" My Mam started wailing, and all the women and Uncle Harold started crying, and I started crying myself as well.

"Can't you do anything to save our Specs, Esther?" my Mam kept on asking her, and after a bit Esther Lee told her, "Yes, I can save him, and I can save all the others as well. But it will cost you some money. I have to buy things to sacrifice to the maid."

"Oh, my God! I've already spent the housekeeping money this week." My Mam was really upset. "I can give you some money next Friday when I gets me wages."

Hilda only had a shilling, and Doreen and Mrs Polson hadn't got any money. Nor had Uncle Harold.

"We'll give you the money next Friday when we gets our wages," they all promised.

Esther Lee shook her head and looked all doubtful. "It could be too late then. The maid usually takes her victim very quick after she's appeared."

My Mam run upstairs and searched through Uncle Sid's stuff, but she couldn't find any money there. She even asked Granny Smith, but she's having one of her funny turns again and she's been in bed for ages and when my Mam asked her if she'd got any money, all she said was, "I've got a thousand pounds hid away."

"Hid away where, Mam?" my Mam asked her.

"It's hid away up Jack's arse, hanging on a nail," Granny Smith told her. "It's been up there for 50 years."

"I'll tell you what I'll do," Esther Lee offered. "You can give me the ration coupons for next week, and I'll take them to somebody I know who'll give me something for them. But mind you all keep quiet about it, because I could get put in jail for doing this for you. And I'm only doing it to save this poor little cratur's life and the lives of the other poor little craturs that the maid has come to get."

They all fetched their ration books and they give Esther Lee the coupons she wanted.

"Right," she told us all. "I'm going to save the chaveys from the maid. Don't let them out of the house until after six o'clock tomorrow morning. Not even to go to the lavatory. After six o'clock tomorrow morning they'll be safe, and you can let them out then. I shall have made the sacrifice to the maid by then, and she'll have gone back to the shadowy land beyond the grave."

The grown-ups was ever so grateful to Esther Lee, but I thought it was a bit of a swiz taking all the sweet coupons like she did. I won't be able to have a sweet for ages, will I? It aren't fair!

Chapter Twenty-Seven

Mr Cook's monkey, the one that bit Johnny Merry's finger, run away the other night, and it got on the roof of the church down town and it give the vicar a heart attack and he had to go to the hospital. Mrs Masters, who lives on the other side of our house to Mrs Savin, come in to tell my Mam all about it. Mrs Masters' sister, Edith, lives next door to Mr Cook and his monkey, you see, so she knows everything that goes on in that street and she tells Mrs Masters all the news.

Well, the monkey run away in the middle of the night, Mrs Masters said, and my Mam said, "How did it get out of its cage in the middle of the night?"

Mrs Masters winked at her. "The dirty old bastard takes it out of the cage every night, Effie."

I was having my supper. A bowl of Oxo with some bread broke up in it, it's ever so nice. And I asked Mrs Masters, "Does Mr Cook take the monkey out of the cage to take it for a walk?"

"Yes, Chucky Face!" Mrs Masters was roaring laughing.

"Where does he take it to? Does he take it down the cemetery like Mr Bent takes his dog?"

"No, Chucky Face, he takes it for a walk up the wooden

hills to Bedfordshire." Mrs Masters kept on laughing, and my Mam told her, "You shouldn't tell him things like that, Mary. He'll go blabbing it all over the place."

"It don't matter a bugger if he does, Effie, because it's the truth. The dirty old bastard ought to be strung up for it. It's a bloody disgrace, so it is."

Mrs Masters looked as if she was getting mad for a minute and then my Mam grinned and asked Mrs Masters, "Shouldn't they ask the monkey what it wants doing with him though, Mary? It might upset it to see its husband dangling from the gallows."

And Mrs Masters told her, "Well, if they does hang him, it'll just be one more poor widow weeping around the town, won't it?"

"Will Mrs Cook be crying when Mr Cook gets hung then, Mam?" I asked her, "Because Johnny Merry told me that Mrs Cook didn't like Mr Cook and that was why she run away with a Chinaman."

"Shurrup pestering me, and get your supper ate. It's time you was up the wooden hill yourself," my Mam shouted, and she chased me upstairs and made me get into bed.

When I went to school in the morning all the kids was talking about Mr Cook's monkey getting on the church roof and giving the vicar a heart attack. They said that the vicar, who's ever so big and fat, was up in the tower looking at the bells when the monkey poked its head through the window and the vicar shrieked because he thought that it was the devil come to get him. They said the vicar run down the stairs and out into the road and he was shouting, "Get thee behind me, Satan!"

And then the monkey run after him and jumped on his back, and he had his heart attack then. But he didn't die or anything, because a copper run up and carried him to the hospital, and now he's laying in bed and he's got sweets and comics all round him piled up high that the church people has brought him.

After that the monkey climbed back up onto the church roof and the fire engine come out, and the Home Guards with their rifles, because they thought that it was a Jerry paratrooper.

Rita Spencer, who's my sweetheart only she won't talk to me because she says I'm scruffy and ugly, told us that she was walking past with her Mam and Dad when the Home Guards was firing their guns at the monkey, and Johnny Merry said ever so quick, "It's a good job your Dad had his hat on, else the Home Guards would have fired at him as well, because he looks like a monkey."

Rita Spencer run and told Miss Brown that Johny Merry had called her Dad a monkey, and Miss Brown come roaring after him, and she copped him just as he was climbing over the school wall and she didn't half give him a clout. Then she kept hold of him and sent Rita Spencer to fetch her cane from the office. When Rita Spencer brought the cane Miss Brown got Johnny Merry by the scruff of his neck and bent him over and give him a tanning with the cane. He went all red in the face, but he didn't cry because he's tough.

Then, when she was all tired out and had to let him go while she got her breath back, he told her, "That didn't hurt a bit."

And he run off, and she was too tired to run after him, and Miss Ladwood's only got one lung, and she's all old and bent over, so she couldn't run after him neither.

Then Miss Brown got us all lined up and told us, "Now, children, we are all going to join in a prayer for the return to health of the vicar, because he is a truly good and saintly man, and that wicked monkey is an agent of the Devil, who was sent by Satan himself to give the poor vicar a heart attack."

We had to stand there for ages while Miss Brown prayed.

When I got home I told my Mam about us praying for the vicar, and I told her that Miss Brown said that Satan himself had give the vicar his heart attack.

My Mam sniffed ever so loud and said all snotty-like, "It aren't Satan who gave the hypocritical old bugger the heart attack. It's all the bloody port wine and pheasants he keeps getting down his gullet. More power to Satan's elbow, that's what I says, and I hope he sends a gorilla to jump on the fat old bugger's back the next time."

My Mam don't like the vicar, you know, because he stopped her down town one day and told her that she ought to be ashamed of herself for living in sin like she was doing.

When she come home and told Hilda what the vicar had said to her, my Mam was ever so mad, but Hilda only laughed and told her, "Nobody can say that you'm living in sin with Sidney Tompkins, my duck. You aren't living in sin! You'm only carrying out an act of true Christian charity to take that scrawny, scruffy bugger into your bed."

"Oh, that's very funny, I'm sure," my Mam said, all

snotty-like, and she sulked for ages after that. Anyway, the monkey stopped up on top of the church roof until it got hungry, and one of the firemen brought some conkers to give it, and it come down and they copped it in a net.

"I didn't know that monkeys eat conkers," my Mam told Mrs Masters, and Mrs Masters was roaring with laughing again, and she said, "No, they don't eat conkers, Effie, they eats bananas. They sucks the flesh out of the skins."

"Well, where the hell does Old Cook get hold of bananas to give to the bloody monkey to suck?" my Mam wanted to know, and Mrs Masters fell off her chair laughing.

"It aren't a banana he gives it, Effie, it only looks like a banana and the bloody silly monkey don't know the difference."

I've never had a banana, you know. What I'd like to know is why a monkey gets bananas and not a kid? It aren't fair, is it?

Chapter Twenty-Eight

The man on the wireless said that the Jerries was sending rockets over which was blowing up lots of things. He said that they was a new sort, not like the Doodlebugs that was coming over before. Uncle Sid said that he was the one who showed our pilots how to deal with the Doodlebugs. He said that what he done was to fly along in his plane and when he saw a Doodlebug he'd fly up to it and use his wings to turn it round so it went back to Germany and fell on Berlin. Uncle Sid said that's why Adolf Hitler had to make this new rocket because, thanks to Uncle Sid, the Doodlebugs was no good to him any more. Uncle Sid says that Adolf Hitler has declared him 'Public Enemy Number One', and that if the Jerries had come to England then him and Winston Churchill would have been shot at dawn because Adolf Hitler knows that him and Winston Churchill are an inspiration to the British people. Uncle Sid says that Adolf Hitler told his men, "As long as Sidney Tompkins and Winston Churchill are alive, the British will never surrender. If we can get them two, then we shall win the war."

Uncle Harold was stood scratching Granny Smith's back and listening to what Uncle Sid was telling me. Granny Smith is all better again now, you know. At least that's what my Mam says. But Granny Smith seems just the same to me. I can't tell the difference between her being all better or when she's having one of her funny turns. I don't think Uncle Harold likes it when Granny Smith is all better though, because then he has to scratch her back, and when she's having one of her funny turns, he don't have to scratch it.

Anyway, Uncle Harold said ever so nice, "Tell me, Sidney, when exactly did Adolf Hitler make that speech to the Reichstag? Do you know the date?"

Uncle Sid stared all suspicious-like at him. "Why does you want to know, Harold?"

"Because I want to incorporate it into my memoirs, Sidney. Into the volume that deals with the war years. I'm sure that a speech like that has been widely recorded, and I'd like to read the full text in its entirety. I don't want to quote any passages which may be out of context with the essential import of the speech. Adolf Hitler has considerable relevance to this war, and I cannot afford to misquote him. Posterity would not appreciate that."

Uncle Harold is talking all posh now because he's been promoted at work, and he uses a lot of long words that I don't know what they means. I don't reckon Uncle Sid knows what the long words means neither, because he told Uncle Harold all snappy, "Mind your own business. It's got nothing to do with you. You just get on with your scratching. That's about all you'm good for."

Hilda come in just as he said that and she flew at him. "I'll have you know that my Harold has been promoted to a very important position in the undertaking profession. So he's good for a lot more than you'll ever be good for, Sidney Tompkins. Smiling Sam says that my Harold is the jewel in the crown and the finest flower in the wreath of the undertaking world."

"Phwhattt?" Uncle Sid was ever so scornful. "He's the liveliest bugger in the cemetery, more like. And that aren't hard to be, is it, seeing as all the other buggers down there are dead."

"Don't bother bandying words with him, Hilda, my dearest darling," Uncle Harold said all lofty-like. "He is merely a Philistine, and as such is beneath our consideration. We have far more important matters to concern ourselves with. Now that I've become Smiling Sam's Director of Burial Music and Ceremony, I really do not have the time, or the patience, or the inclination to engage in disputations with him."

"Hark at it?" Uncle Sid did his sarcastic look. "He's calls himself Director of Burial Music and Ceremony. What bloody music does he mean? There's bloody Tommy TeeTee with a tambourine, and Bertie Shellshock with a bloody tin drum, and Lord Muck here poncing along in front of them waving a broomstick like he's a bloody Drum Major, and the silly buggers who're paying for it all marching along behind the coffin. The only one who looks as if he's enjoying it all is the one in the bloody coffin."

"That's just goes to show what you knows about it," Hilda told him. "You knows bugger-all. Everybody says that the new War Funeral ceremony is the most moving thing that they've ever seen. And that when Tommy TeeTee and Bertie Shellshock plays the 'Last Post' as the coffin is being lowered into the grave, and my Harold stands at attention and salutes, then it brings tears to their eyes, it's all so beautiful and moving."

197

"Oh yes! The 'Last Post' sounds smashing being played on the tambourine, don't it?" Uncle Sid was all triumphant. "And when Tommy TeeTee was so drunk that when he went to hit his tambourine he missed it and fell over into the grave on top of the coffin, that was all beautiful and moving, wasn't it? And how about when they played the 'Trumpet Voluntary' on the tambourine and drum, and your Harold had to pretend that he was the bloody trumpet and make all the noises with his mouth. That was ever so beautiful and moving."

And then, before Hilda could think of anything to say, Uncle Sid jumped up and told her, "I rest my case." Then he went out laughing all scornful.

My Mam come in then and said that she was going to make 'War and Peace Pudding' with carrot fudge because a woman at work at given her the recipes for them.

I hates carrots, you know. There's posters all over the place with pictures of 'Potato Pete' and 'Doctor Carrot' on them, saying 'Eat me.'

My Mam got all the stuff for the 'War and Peace Pudding' and she showed me how to make it. She got some flour and some breadcrumbs and some suet. Then she got some raw carrots and cut them up all small like shavings, and some dried currants. Then she got some bicarbonate of soda. That's horrible, that is. She makes me drink it sometimes in hot water. Oh, it makes me all bitter in me mouth and makes me shiver. Well, she mixed everything together and put it into a bowl and then she steamed it like it was a proper jam rolypoly. Then she got a bit of sugar and some treacle and some more carrot shavings and made the carrot fudge with them. It was horrible! And the 'War and Peace Pudding' was horrible as well.

But Uncle Harold ate all his up ever so quick, and he ate what I left as well. He said it was ambrosia, whatever that is.

My Mam told him not to use language like that in front of me and Virgy.

After I had my dinner I went out to play. Me and Johnny Merry are going to make some racing trolleys. What we does is to get hold of some pram wheels, and then we gets a plank of wood and some other bits of wood and we builds a trolley. The bigger the wheels, the faster the trolley goes. But it's ever so hard finding the wheels, because all the kids wants trolleys. It's the craze now. I wonder who makes the crazes? Because some weeks it's a craze for cigarette cards, and other weeks it's conkers, then marbles, then Jacky Five Stones, and then we has stilts and walking cans and hoops, and different games on different weeks. One craze that lasted for ages was playing at 'D-Day'. Letty Dobbs' dad was at D-Day, because he's a commando. Letty says that he was the first one to hit the beach and that he killed hundreds of Jerries. The commandos wears a green beret, you know, and the paratroopers wears a red beret, and the tankies wears a black beret. I likes the red beret the best, because I'm going to be a paratrooper like Frankie Savin. I like Frankie Savin again now, because when he got better he was all laughing and jolly again, like he was before. His Mam told me that Frankie was in the D-Day as well. He jumped out of a plane and when he was coming down on his parachute he was shooting the Jerries with his tommy-gun. I should like to have seen him doing that.

Letty Dobbs has the same crazes as the rest of our gang, but the other girls don't have many crazes. They just skips all the time, they gets long pieces of rope and they takes turns and going in and out of the skipping. They sings a lot of stuff while they're skipping as well. I know some of the things they sings. There's one that goes:

> *'Oner, twoer, three and four,*
> *Charlie Chaplin went to war.*
> *He taught the ladies how to dance,*
> *And this is what he taught them.*
> *Heel, toe, over you go,*
> *Heel, toe, over you go,*
> *Salute to the King,*
> *And bow to the Queen,*
> *And turn your back on the submarine."*

That's good, aren't it? And there's another one I know, as well:

> *Rin Tin Tin he swallowed a pin*
> *He went to the doctor,*
> *The doctor wasn't in.*
> *He knocked on the door,*
> *And fell through the floor,*
> *And that was the end of Rin Tin Tin.*

There's sometimes I wouldn't mind doing skipping with the girls. Like when Rita Spencer is skipping in the playground at school. Rita Spencer is my sweetheart, only she don't like me. But boys can't skip with girls. Only sissies can skip with the girls, and our gang's tough, so we can't skip with the girls. But I'd still like to skip with Rita Spencer sometimes.

Rin Tin Tin is a dog, you know. He's a film star as well. I saw a serial once at the pictures with Hopalong Cassidy in it and he had a dog, only it wasn't Rin Tin Tin. I saw Roy Rogers and Trigger the Wonder Horse as well at the pictures. And Lassie. Lassie's a dog who is clever like we are. Uncle Sid says that Lassie is a sight cleverer than most human beings, because Lassie gets paid millions of pounds for working and human beings gets paid next to nothing.

Johnny Merry played ever such a good joke once on Miss Brown at school. He got an old biscuit tin and he brought it to school and when we was all in class he told Miss Brown, "Please Miss, can I show you my tin."

And she said, all snotty, "Why should I be interested in seeing that dirty old tin, Merry?"

And then he told her, ever so quick, "Because it's the tin that Rin Tin Tin shit in, Miss."

She come roaring across the desks and she copped hold of him, and she dragged him into the lavatories and she washed his mouth out with carbolic soap and water. It made him ever so sick. He told me that every night for a week after that he woke up blowing millions of bubbles out of his mouth, and the bubbles went floating all across the ceiling, and filled all the house, and the bubbles got into his big sister Doreen's eyes and made them smart and she fell down the stairs because her eyes was smarting so bad that she couldn't see where she was.

I told my Mam what had happened to Doreen, and she said, "It wasn't bubbles that made her eyes smart."

201

And Hilda laughed, and said, "I should be so lucky."

"And me, and all!" my Mam said, and then she laughed as well.

They don't half say some daft things sometimes, my Mam and Hilda does.

Chapter Twenty-Nine

We saw some Jerries yesterday. Some real ones, not at the pictures. They come in lorries to the fields on the other side of the railway line. Some of them was wearing Africa Corps caps and there was soldiers with real tommy-guns guarding them. All the kids went down to see them. Johnny Merry did his Adolf Hitler imitation, and when he was goose-stepping up and down one of the soldiers with the tommy-guns, he was old with grey hair and he had a lot of medal ribbons on his coat, well he come across and clouted Johnny Merry right on his earhole. He knocked Johnny Merry flying, and Johnny Merry got up and shouted, "What did you do that for? I was only playing."

And the soldier told him, "I've been fighting these blokes through two wars, you little bleeder, and I've got respect for them. If I catch you trying to take the piss again, I'll knock you into next week. Now sod off, the lot of you!"

But we didn't go. What we did was run away a bit, and then come round on the other side of the Jerries where the old soldier couldn't see us.

The Jerries had picks and shovels and they started to dig long trenches, and while they was doing that some other Jerries was building big huts with wooden planks and tin roofs.

"What's you building, Mister? Is it a camp?" Fatty Polson shouted to one of the soldiers, and the soldier told him,

"It's a prison camp, and you're going to be put in it if you don't bugger off."

They wasn't half miserable those soldiers. And the Jerries was as well. They never smiled or laughed or anything, they just looked all sour faced at us. Not like the Ities who works on the dustcart. The Ities on the dustcart are always singing and laughing and shouting to the women, and when they sees us they sometimes tells us, "Chow Bambinos."

My Mam told me that that's Italian and it means "Hello Babbies!"

Well, I don't like being called a babby, because I'm big now. But I don't expect the Ities knows how old I am, does they, so that's why they calls us Babbies in Italian. I like the Ities though, because they sings and laughs a lot.

I asked Uncle Sid why the Ities was laughing, and the Jerries was all miserable, and he said, "It's because the Jerries are real soldiers and don't like being beat. The Ities don't mind being beat, because they'll never be real soldiers as long as they've still got holes in their arses. They're bloody useless. I used to take hundreds of them prisoners when I was out in the desert."

My Mam was doing the ironing and she heard what Uncle Sid told me, and she went all snotty. "If you ask me, the Ities have got the right idea. They'd sooner be laughing and singing, rather than fighting and dying."

Uncle Sid stared at her like he was surprised, and then

he said, all sarcastic, "Well, excuse me Madam, but I don't recollect asking you. And I don't recollect anyone else asking you, neither."

"Oh, is that so!" My Mam was getting mad, I could tell, because when she gets mad all her throat goes red, and she slits her eyes, and she slams things down hard.

Well, she took the iron off the fire, and instead of wiping it like she always does with a damp rag, she only slammed it down on the table, on top of Uncle Sid's best white shirt that she was going to iron for him, so he could wear it to go out to the pub. All smoke and fire come off the shirt and Uncle Sid shouted, "Look what you've been and gone and done now, you silly cow!"

And he jumped up and picked up his shirt and there was a big hole burned right through it, and he looked through the hole at my Mam, and she said, "Oh Sid, you look like a real picture in a frame, so you do. A proper portrait." And she sat down on the chair and put her hands on her face and laughed and laughed and laughed, and Uncle Sid was swearing and cussing and stamping up and down looking through the hole in his shirt. And then Hilda and Uncle Harold come in and said that there was a copper outside who was asking who owned the rabbits.

I forgot to tell you about what happened to the rabbits, didn't I? Well, after they all escaped they went to live in different places down our street. A lot of them went to live in the Hostel gardens, and some went to live in Mr Jones-Evans' garden, and the others went all over the place. There's millions of them now, and the neighbours aren't half moaning about them because they eats all the stuff in the gardens, and they makes burrows and holes in the grass and the flower beds. Some of them dug a hole in our back garden, and Uncle Sid set some snares to catch them, but the only thing he caught was our cat. It was nearly strangled but Hilda found it just in time and let it go. She didn't half tell Uncle Sid off about it, and my Mam told him off as well, because she said that he done it on purpose because he don't like our cat. She had some more kittens last week, you know. She had um on the pillow on Uncle Sid's side of the bed. It didn't half make a mess on the pillow, and my Mam had to chuck it away. Uncle Sid was ever so upset about it, because he said that it was the pillow his sainted mother's head had laid on when she died, and that he treasured it for the happy memories it brought back to him.

"My mother was a saint," he said, all tearful. "And her untimely death broke my heart into pieces. I've never got over losing her."

"You're a bloody liar, Sidney Tompkins!" my Mam shouted. "Because I know for a fact that your mother is alive and well and keeping a brothel in West Bromwich. She was in court only last week for living on immoral earnings. It was in all the bloody papers."

Uncle Sid went all red then, and he just mumbled something under his breath.

"What's a brothel, Mam?" I asked her.

"It's a home for soiled doves," she told me.

Well, I know what a dove is. It's a bird that looks like a pigeon. But I don't know what soiled means, so I asked her.

"It means dirty," she said, and then lost her temper and shouted at me to bugger off out and play.

Uncle Sid's Mam must be a nice woman though, mustn't she, being kind and keeping a home for birds with dirt on them. But I wonder why Uncle Sid said that his Mam had died? Perhaps he had two Mams, and one of them has died. I know a kid in our school whose got two Mams. Only one of them is called his Foster-Mam, and the other is called his Natural Mam. That's what Miss Ladwood called her anyway.

Anyway, the copper come to our house and he said he wanted to see Uncle Sid, because somebody down the street had told him that Uncle Sid was the owner of the rabbits.

"I don't own no bloody rabbits," Uncle Sid told him.

Our Virgy was listening, and she said, "Oh, Uncle Sid, don't you know that it's a sin to tell a lie? God hears everything, you know. He'll be angry with you for telling a lie."

Our Virgy is the one who's got the Holy Shrine in our back yard. She's very holy herself and she goes to Sunday School twice on every Sunday, and twice in the week as well.

Then our Virgy told the copper, "Uncle Sid kept the rabbits in the hutch down the back garden, and they all got out one day and run off because he was going to kill them."

"Sweet Jesus Christ!" Uncle Sid sort of gasped out, and Virgy told him, "That's another sin you've just committed, Uncle Sid. Taking the Name of Our Saviour in vain. You need to be washed in the Blood of the Lamb to make your soul white and pure again."

"And you needs to be bloody well boiled in oil." Uncle Sid was all ratty with her, but the copper smiled at her and told her, "You're a good girl for telling the truth, and I shall make sure that I write that down in my report."

Virgy was all pleased with herself then, and sat smiling and looking ever so smug. She's horrible and sneaky, our Virgy is. I don't like her. Nor her friends neither. They'm all horrible and sneaky as well.

"Now, Mr Tompkins, there have been twenty-three complaints made against you because it's your rabbits that's causing damage to peoples' properties." The copper started reading out names from his book, and when he was reading them out, Uncle Sid kept on scowling and telling him, "I don't own no bloody rabbits. I don't own no bloody rabbits. How can I own the bloody rabbits when they all run off and left me? They declared their independence, didn't they. Well, the bloody Yanks declared their independence as well, didn't they, and we don't own America any more, does we. So how the hell can I own the bloody rabbits after they run off and declared their independence. It's the bloody rabbits you should be talking to, not me."

"Uncle Sid, don't you know that it's a sin to swear," Virgy told him. "Every time God hears you make a swear word, he puts a black mark on your soul."

"I don't bloody well care if he throws a pot of bloody black tar on my bloody soul," Uncle Sid shouted, and the copper looked all stern at him, and told him, "Now then, now then, I shall have to arrest you if you keep on offering abuse to this child."

"Offering abuse?" Uncle Sid stared at him all amazed. "You'm talking out the top of your bloody daft helmet, mate."

"That's it!" The copper lost his temper then. "You're under arrest, my lad, for offering abuse to a police officer."

And he grabbed Uncle Sid by his collar and he dragged him off to the police station.

"Bloody hell!" Uncle Sid shouted, and Virgy told him, "That's two swear words you just made Uncle Sid, so two more black marks are on your soul. You needs to be washed in the Blood of the Lamb."

Then she went to her Holy Shrine in the back yard to pray to God to have mercy on such a wicked sinner like Uncle Sid.

When Uncle Sid come back from the police station he was all pitiful and sorry for himself, and he sat at the table in our kitchen and told my Mam, "I'm sick to death of my rotten life, Effie. For two bloody pins I'd end it all."

Hilda heard him say that and quick as a flash she pulled some hairpins out from under her turban and give them to him.

"Here's three pins," she told him. "The extra one's to make sure you does a good job of it."

But my Mam was sorry for him, and told him, "Cheer up, my duck. What did the coppers say to you anyway?"

"They says that I've got to get rid of the bloody rabbits in double quick time, else they'll get somebody to do it and I'll have to pay for whoever they gets, as well as pay for all the damage that the rabbits has done up to now."

"What?" My Mam skreeked at him. "Am you telling me that you've got to pay for the damage that the rabbits has done already?"

"That's what the coppers told me." Uncle Sid looked like he was going to cry.

"Hilda, fetch that bloody clothes line in from the back yard," my Mam shouted. "I'm going to help this daft silly bugger to hang himself."

209

"It aren't summat to laugh about, Effie." Uncle Sid was all indignant.

My Mam's throat was red again, and her eyes was all slitted. "Who's bloody well laughing, Sidney Tompkins?" she sort of hissed like a snake at him.

Gordy Alpern, that's a kid from down the bottom of the Hill, he's got some snakes, you know. They're called grass snakes and sometimes he brings them to school with him, and chases the girls with them. He chases the little kids as well, because they'm all fritted of the snakes. Gordy Alpern tells the little kids and the girls that the snakes am poisonous, and when the snakes sinks their fangs into them they'll shrivel up and turn black and die within seconds, and the girls and the little kids all believes him, so that's why they'm so fritted of his snakes.

Me and Johnny Merry don't like Gordy Alpern. None of our gang likes him, because he's nasty and he stinks. Me and Johnny Merry aren't fritted of his snakes, because we knows that they're not poisonous. You see, we goes snake hunting ourselves down on the Red Banks where the snakes likes to live, and we knows the difference between vipers and adders and grass snakes and slow worms.

The last time Gordy Alpern brought his snakes to school he had a real big one down his trousers, and when it was playtime he started to chase the girls and the little kids, and there's one little kid who's a blue babby, and aren't ever very well, but he's a nice kid. His lips am ever so blue and his face as well, and he can only walk slow because he can't breathe proper. My Mam says that it's his heart that's all wonky, and she says it's only God's mercy that

210

he's still alive. Well, Gordy Alpern chased him with the big snake and the little kid started to cry because he can't run away like the other kids can, because he's a blue babby with a wonky heart, so me and Johnny Merry went and got Gordy Alpern, and we took the big long snake off him and we tied it into lots of knots, until it was just one big granny knot, and then we played football with it.

Gordy Alpern run off crying to fetch his Mam, and she come roaring into the playground just as Johnny Merry scored a goal with the snake ball.

Gordy Alpern's Mam is ever so tough, everybody down the Hill is fritted of her. One day she had a fight with some Gyppoes and beat up six of them all at once. She's all big and fat and her hair is always in curlers, and she's only got a couple of teeth in her mouth and they'm all long and snaggly and black, and her eyes are red and squashed up tight together, and she's got a moustache. Mrs Masters calls her the 'Cave Woman', and says that she's a throwback from the Stone Age. She says that Mrs Alpern's breath kills flies at twenty paces, and that strong men grow weak and tremble when she approaches them. My Mam says that Mrs Alpern got her husband by going out with a big stone club and hitting him over the head with it and dragging him back to her house by his hair. But I reckon that my Mam is just being daft when she says that because I saw Mr Alpern one day when he took his cap off, and he hadn't got hardly no hair at all on his head. He was all baldy. So Mrs Alpern couldn't have dragged him back to her house by his hair, could she?

I told my Mam that, and she said, "Well, you see, Specs, it's like this. When Mrs Alpern caught Mr Alpern the first time, he had a lot of hair on his head. Only when she was dragging him back to her house some of his hair got pulled out. Well, ever since then he keeps on running away from her, so she keeps on going after him and hitting him over the head with her club and dragging him back to the house by his hair. Well, every time she does that a bit more hair gets pulled out of his head by the roots. He's run away and been dragged back so many times, that now the poor bugger arn't got hardly a hair left on his head at all."

"Well, how can she still drag him back to her house then?" I asked her, and Hilda laughed and said, "She grabs hold of his willie and pulls him along by that."

And my Mam skreeked out laughing. "That's why Mr Alpern always talks so squeaky-voiced, Specs. Just look how big the little sod's eyes have got, will you, Hilda. They'm like bloody saucers. He'll be the death of me."

And they both went on roaring with laughing for ages and ages.

Anyway, Mrs Alpern come roaring into the playground just as Johnny Merry scored a goal, only Mrs Alpern was coming through our goal posts when he scored. They'm not really goal posts, they'm the school gates. The snake hit Mrs Alpern right in her chops, and some of it went right into her mouth because she was shouting at us.

We all started to run away, and we climbed up on the big wall, and because she's so big and fat Mrs Alpern couldn't climb up after us. She was stamping up and down underneath us, cussing and shouting and swearing at us, and she kept on waving her fists at us and telling us, "I'm going to kill you little bastards! I'm going to tear your bleedin' yeds right off your bleedin' shoulders and shove 'um up your bleedin' arses!"

And Johnny Merry started to laugh at her, and he

kept on shouting, "Just come on up here if you wants a fight, Fatty."

And she went mad then, and she picked up the ball of snake and threw it at him. Only it missed him and hit me instead, and knocked me right off the wall. I landed right on me head and cut it open, and it didn't half hurt, and it was all bleeding.

I run home and told my Mam what had happened, and she clouted me for climbing onto the wall, and then, after she'd put a plaster on my head, she give me another tanning for being cruel to the snake. But you can't be cruel to snakes, can you? They can't feel anything, everybody knows that. Johnny Merry didn't get a tanning, did he? It arn't fair!

Well, as I said, when Uncle Sid told my Mam that the coppers said he had to pay for all the damage that the rabbits had done, she was mad at first, but then she sat down and had a think.

"I reckon there might be a way we can do ourselves a bit of good, Sid," she told him. "But we've got to box clever."

"What shall we do, Effie?" Uncle Sid was looking all hopeful.

My Mam smiled, all sly. "We're going to spread a rumour, Sid. We're going to spread it about that one of them rabbits ate a very valuable diamond ring that was left to my Mam by her great grandmother. And that the ring is worth thousands of pounds."

"Poooh, that's no bloody good, Effie," Uncle Sid told her, all scornful. "Who's going to believe that your family owned a very valuable ring worth thousands of pounds? Everybody knows that your family has never even owned a pot to piss in."

My Mam got snotty with him then. "Oh, is that so? Well let me tell you summat, Mister Smartarse Knowitall. My Great Uncle Tom went to Alaska when the Gold Rush was on, and he found a gold mine and made millions of pounds out of it. Everybody knows that."

"And everybody knows that he never ever come back to this country, and he never so much as sent a bloody crumb of gold back to you lot. He never ever wrote to you, did he? Let alone shared his millions of pounds with you."

"That's all you knows." My Mam looked all mysterious at him. "You see, what we shall say, is that we never spoke about the ring he sent to us, because we was afraid that we might have burglars, and we was waiting until the war is over before we was going to sell it, because then we'd get a better price for it."

Uncle Sid thought about that for a bit, and then he sort of nodded. "You might have summat there, Effie."

"Listen, you just leave it all to me, and say nothing to nobody," my Mam told him ever so strict. "Leave it all to me, and keep that big mouth of yours tight shut."

There's a woman who lives up the top of our row who none of the grown-ups likes, because they says that she's the nosiest old cow in Christendom. They says that she's got the biggest mouth in England, and that if you wants the world to know all your business, then just tell it to her. She's called Clara the Clarion, because the newspaper is called 'The Clarion', and they says that she's better than the newspaper for spreading the news. Mrs Masters says that the government could save millions and millions of pounds if they closed all the wireless stations down and just told Clara the Clarion what was going on, because she'd broadcast it to everybody in record time. But even when everybody says that they don't like her, they always seems to be calling to her, and whispering with her in corners of the street. Grown-ups are ever so false like that, aren't they. Because when us kids don't like somebody, we don't talk to them, but grown-ups does and smiles as well.

What my Mam did was write a letter and she took it and dropped it in the entry just before Clara the Clarion come home from work. Then she told me, "Listen, Specs, whatever anybody asks you in the next few days, you just tell them that you don't know nothing."

"But what if it's about summat that I does know, Mam?"

Her throat started to get red. "You knows nothing about nothing, Specs. I shan't tell you again. Now get to bed."

When my Mam talks like that, all sort of tight-lipped and snarly, then I never answers her back, because she tans me if I does. So I don't know nothing about nothing now.

Chapter Thirty

We're going fishing for tiddlers next Saturday. Me and Johnny Merry and Fatty Polson and the rest of the gang. We always goes fishing for tiddlers to Bantry Brook. It's ever such a long way to go, and we have to go through the woods and over the fields. The woods are on the other side of the golf course where all the posh people plays golf. Sometimes we goes over the golf course to get to the woods but then the posh people shouts at us and chases us off. The posh people don't like us kids, you know, because we plays tricks on them. What we does is hide in the bushes and when the golf ball comes rolling by us, we jumps out and picks it up and then runs off with it and hides in the bushes again. They don't half swear and cuss when they comes to look for their balls and they can't find them. Another joke we plays is when the ball comes by us we picks it up and throws it into the sandpits. It's ever so funny to watch the men trying to hit the ball when it's in the sand. The sand keeps on flying up all over the place, and the men gets ever so mad and sweaty.

One man once was looking for his ball, and me and Johnny Merry was hiding in the bushes with it, and the man looked all around him, and when he saw that the other men he was playing with was coming along towards him, he took another golf ball out of his pocket and dropped it by his feet, and when the other men come up he told them, "I say, you chaps, this was a stroke of luck, wasn't it? My ball is just right for the green. I'm going to get an eagle on this hole."

Posh people talks like that, don't they, all sort of funny like. We looked all over but we couldn't see an eagle anywhere. Perhaps he got mixed up and he meant a magpie or a blackbird or something, because there was lots of them sorts of birds flying around.

And then Johnny Merry jumped out of the bushes and told the man, "Here's your ball, Mister. It run into the bushes and we saw it so we went to find it for you."

The man went all red and he told us, "That's not my ball."

"Yes it is, Mister, because we saw when you hit it, and we watched it come all the way, didn't we, Specs?"

And I said, "Yes, Mister, we watched it come all the way and roll into the bushes."

The man went even redder then, and he sort of gritted his teeth so that they went all grindy and he looked like he was grinning, only he wasn't grinning, if you know what I mean. Then he told us, "Now just be good boys and run along with you. That isn't my ball. This is my ball, this ball at my feet here. The ball you have in your filthy little paw is someone else's ball."

"No, it's not, Mister," Johnny Merry told him. "It's your ball, because we watched you hit it and it come down there and it rolled into the bushes. Didn't it, Specs?"

"Yes, Mister. We watched it come down after you hit it, and it run into the bushes."

Then the other men all sort of frowned at each other,

and one of them said, ever so snotty-like, "They do seem to be convinced that they have your ball, Osmond."

And Johnny Merry told him, "It is his ball, Mister. And that's his ball as well, on the ground by his feet. Because we saw him pull it out of his pocket and drop it there, didn't we, Specs?"

"Yeah, we saw him do that, Mister," I told the man. "He took it out of his pocket while you was walking up here, and he dropped it on the ground there."

The other men looked ever so fierce then, and they all turned to look at the first man, and he swore at me and Johnny Merry and he threw his golf club at us. If we hadn't of ducked ever so quick it would have knocked our heads off, I'm sure.

Then all the men started to fight, they was punching and kicking and swearing and cussing at each other, and me and Johnny Merry run off in case they started on us next. But we didn't half laugh at the things they was shouting at each other. Really rude names and everything. I never knew that the posh people knew all them rude names before.

When we goes fishing for tiddlers we makes fishing nets out of canes and wire and bits of old sacks. We catches red soldiers and sticklebacks. The red soldiers are the best because they're all shiny and red down their chests. The sticklebacks are all right, but they aren't coloured so nice. We takes jam jars with us to bring the fishes home in, and when we brings them home we feeds them on worms and dead flies, but my fishes always seems to die quick. So when they dies I give them to our cat to eat. Another thing we catches is newts. We gets them out of the big Air Raid tank down by the Grammar

School. The tank is all filled with water, you see, to put the fires out with when the Jerries bombs us and sets the houses on fire.

Uncle Sid used to have to do fire-watching at the factory he works at. He said that they give him a bucket of sand, and another bucket for water and a stirrup pump. The bucket of sand was for putting on the incendiary bombs, and the water and pump was for spraying on the fires. Uncle Sid told me that he put the sand on dozens of incendiary bombs, and used the water and pump dozens of times to put out fires that the Jerry bombs started. He said that he got a medal for saving the factory from burning down. He said that the Jerries come over one night and they dropped hundreds of incendiary bombs on his factory and the fires started everywhere. He said that the other fire watchers got fritted and run away, but he put sand on all the bombs, and squirted water on all the fires and put them out. He said that the boss of the factory told Winston Churchill, "Thank God that Sidney Tompkins was there. We would have lost the factory else, and without the secret weapons that the factory makes, we would lose the war."

Uncle Sid said that Winston Churchill came to see him at the factory and thanked him personally for being so brave and saving the factory single-handed. And then Winston Churchill give Uncle Sid a medal, and he said to Uncle Sid, "Name your reward, Mr Tompkins, and it shall be yours."

Uncle Sid said that he told Winston Churchill, "Mr Churchill, I already have my reward. And that is the knowledge that I have done my duty for my King and my country."

Uncle Sid said that tears come into Winston Churchill's eyes and rolled down his cheeks, and he told Uncle Sid, "Mr Tompkins, if there were 10,000 men like you we would have won this war long ago. God bless you, Mr Tompkins, and all who sail with you. You have my gratitude and the gratitude of your King and country."

I told Hilda what Winston Churchill had said to Uncle Sid, but she only laughed and told me, "The only bloody fire that Sidney Tompkins ever put out was a fag end that he stamped on. And he only dared to do that because he was drunk at the time."

I told Uncle Sid what Hilda had said, and he looked ever so fierce and he told me, "She's just a jealous cow, because her precious bloody Harold never put out any fires and got given a medal and thanked by Winston Churchill. Don't you believe a word she tells you, Specs. You just listen to me, then you'll know what's what."

I asked Uncle Sid to show me his medal, but he said he couldn't, because it was with all his other medals at Buckingham Palace. He said that the King and Queen and Winston Churchill likes to show people his medals, because it proves that it's us that's winning the war, and not the bleedin' Yanks.

Uncle Sid still don't like the Yanks, you know. He says that they can't fight their way out of paper bags. But Frankie Savin says that Uncle Sid is talking through his arsehole, as per usual. Frankie Savin come back home from Italy the other day, and he's ever so brown, and his hands are all trembly because he's been blown up by a Jerry shell, and he's got to stay at the hospital until he's better. Anyway, Frankie Savin says that the Yanks are just the same as us, and the Russians and the Jerries

221

and the Ities. Frankie Savin says that when the shells are exploding and when somebody is shooting at you, then it don't matter where you comes from, or what nationality you are, you're still fritted to death.

He let me wear his red beret again, but when I told him that I was going to be a paratrooper when I get big, and I'm going to kill hundreds of Jerries, he got all mad and told me that if he had his way the buggers who caused the wars 'ud be made to go and fight them. He said that once this bloody war is over he never wants to think about it again, and he said that he hoped to God that I should never have to wear any colour of beret. He said he'd seen too many good blokes dying and wounded to believe in any more rubbish about fighting for the bloody King and country. He said he'd make the bloody King go and do a bit of fighting himself, and all the bloody politicians and war profiteers with him. They wouldn't be so keen on telling everybody how good and right it was to fight for the King and country then.

I don't like Frankie Savin any more, you know. He's all miserable and sour-faced now. Not like he was when he went to the war. He was all laughing then. I'm still going to be a paratrooper when I get big though.

The last time we went fishing in Bantry Brook we saw Tick Tock the Clockwork Man down there. He was fishing as well. We calls him Tick Tock the Clockwork Man because he walks all stiff and jerky, just like a clockwork man. And he's mad, as well. His eyes are all big and white and he rolls them round and round in his head. He don't bring a jam jar with him when he fishes, because he eats the tiddlers when he catches them in his net. It's true! He does! He eats the tiddlers when he catches them. When he sees us looking at him, he grins and he rolls his eyes round and round and he takes the tiddlers and puts them into his mouth, and then he lets their tails poke out and wriggle, and then he crunches them between his teeth and he chews them up and swallows them. It's true! He does! I've watched him do it hundreds and hundreds of times. Sometimes we gives him our tiddlers to eat as well. He likes Red Soldiers best. He says that they're very tasty. He says that the sticklebacks are allright, but a bit boney.

Johnny Merry give Tick Tock a big newt to eat once, and Tick Tock grinned and rolled his eyes round and round, and he ate the newt, and its tail wasn't half wriggling when he crunched it. But then he asked Johnny Merry, "Where did you get that newt from?"

"From the Grammar School Air Raid tank," Johnny Merry told him, and Tick Tock went mad, and his eyes rolled ever so fast and got all red and bulgy, and he kept on shouting, "I'll kill you, you little bastards! You knows I never ates anything that's had a good education!"

Tick Tock picked up a brick and come after us, and we didn't half run.

But then, the next time we saw him he said to us all nice and smiley, "You arn't got any newts with you, have you, kids? I could just fancy ateing a nice fat newt right now."

They've put a big fence up round the Grammar School Air Raid tank now though. Because a kid fell in and nearly drownded. Some big kids from the Grammar School pulled him out and pumped the water out of him, and he was alright then.

When I told my Mam about the kid falling in and nearly drownding, she asked me, "Was it Johnny Merry?"

And when I told her no, she looked all upset and disappointed, and she looked up at the ceiling and asked, "Why not? Is there no justice to be found at all in this world? Why wasn't it Johnny Merry?"

"Who are you talking to, Mam?" I asked her, because there's nobody on the ceiling, is there? She acts real daft sometimes, my Mam does.

"Anyway, if Johnny Merry fell in the tank he'd get out easy, because he's ever such a good swimmer. He could swim for ages and ages if he fell in," I told her.

"Not if I was there standing on the side of the tank," she said, "with a bloody line prop in me hands. He wouldn't be swimming for ages and ages then."

"Would you pull him out with the line prop, Mam?" I asked her, but all she done was to shake her head ever so slow and look just like Dracula does when he's going to bite his victims' necks and suck their blood from their bodies.

Chapter Thirty-One

There's something funny going on down our street, you know. All the grown-ups are being ever so nice to me, and they're not swearing at Johnny Merry when they sees him with me neither. Today me and Johnny Merry was walking down the street and Mrs Jones-Evans was walking along with her posh friend, Mrs Power. Mrs Power looks a bit like Mrs Jones-Evans, because she always wears her fur coat, even when it's all hot and sunny, and she sweats a lot when it's hot. I know she does because it all runs down her face and makes white lines in her powder and paint.

I told my Mam about Mrs Power having lines running down her face when she sweats, and my Mam sniffed ever so loud and she said, all sort of nasty-like, "It just goes to show, Specs, that it don't matter how many coats of paint you slaps on an old boiler, it still leaks and the rust soon shows through again."

I didn't know what she meant and when I was looking at her, she got all snotty and shouted, "Don't stand there gawping at me, you gormless little bleeder. Now sod off and stop worrying me. If it hadn't been for you I could have had a bloody dozen fur coats. I had me chances until I fell for you."

My Mam's funny like that, you know. Whenever I tells her things about Mrs Jones-Evans and her friends in their fur coats, she always gets mad at me and tells me that she could have had fur coats and big houses and cars and everything if she hadn't had me. Well, I don't reckon that's fair, is it? Because I can't remember stopping her from having all them things, can I?

Well, Mrs Jones-Evans and Mrs Power come walking along the street on the same side as me and Johnny Merry. Now when they does that they just sticks their noses in the air and they walks past us as if we aren't there, only sometimes they pushes us off the pavement and tells us, "Get out of the way, you wretched hooligans!"

They does that when we plays our joke on them. What we does is we gets in front of them and we goes the same way as they does. Only we walks ever so slow, and when they tries to overtake us we pretends that we can't see them and we moves in front of them so that they can't get past. After a bit they gets ever so mad and they always starts off by muttering under their breaths, and then they tells each other that the kids of today arn't got no manners, and then they moans about having to live in the same street as roughs and scruffs, and then the best bit comes, when they goes mad and runs at us and pushes us out of the way. It's the best bit, because then Johnny Merry always digs his heels in and he wriggles and twists so that they can't get a good shove at him, and they gets all breathless and sweaty and they swears at us then.

It's a smashing joke, Johnny Merry showed it me ages ago, and we does it a lot. But you have to be careful who you plays the joke on, because we played it on Mr Reilly when he was coming back from the pub one dinnertime, and he just picked us up by our necks and chucked us over the wall into Mr Lander's back yard. It didn't half hurt when we landed, because we landed on his dog kennel and the dog run out and bit us both. Mr Lander's dog is called Lance, you know. That's a daft name for a dog, arn't it? Lance Landers!

Mr Reilly is Irish, you know. Uncle Sid don't like the Irish. He says that they've all got mud on their boots from the bloody bogs, and that they'm a load of bloody hypocrites because they does bad things all week and then goes to confession on a Sunday and the priest just tells them not to do bad things any more and to say 'Hail Mary' twenty-three times. And then they goes straight out and does bad things all week again until the next Sunday. Uncle Sid says that the Irish hides the Jerry U-boats that sneaks out to sink our ships, and he says that they puts all the lights on at night to show the Jerry bombers the way to go to England.

But my Mam always sticks up for Mr Reilly. She says that he's a decent, hardworking bloke and he can't help being Irish because he couldn't help being born there. And she says that his kids was never so bad as that bad little bugger Johnny Merry is, and he's bloody English, worse luck!

Mr Reilly has got ever such a lot of kids, but they'm all big and grown-up now. Some of them are in the Air Force, and some of them are in the Army, and there's one of them, his name is Gerald, who's in the Marines, and Bridget is in the Women's Army. So whenever Uncle Sid starts carrying on about Mr Reilly and the Irish, my Mam always tells him, "You can say what you like, Sidney Tompkins, but you can't say that the Reilly kids aren't doing their bit in this war. They're doing a bloody sight more than some of the English down this street are doing."

Anyway, Mrs Jones-Evans and Mrs Power was walking down the street on the same side as me and Johnny Merry today, and we thought that we'd play our joke on them. So we started to walk ever so slow, and we could hear their footprints getting closer and closer, only when we moved in front of them, Mrs Jones-Evans smiled at me and she patted my head and told Mrs Power, "This is my little friend, Specs, Amelia. It was his family who introduced all those delightful bunny-rabbits into the street. He's an enchanting child. And this is his little chum, Johnny Merry."

She didn't pat Johnny Merry's head though, or call him an 'enchanting child'.

Then she said, "Would you like a sweetie, Specs?"

"Oooh, yeah!"

"He has beautiful manners, doesn't he, Amelia, despite his poverty. Come along with me then, Specs, and you shall have a sweetie."

I didn't know whether to go with her though, because my Mam always tells me that there are nasty people who come up to kids and asks them if they wants some sweets, and tells them to come along with them and they'll give them sweets. And then, when they gets the kids by themselves they murders them.

My Mam always tells me that if I ever goes off with nasty people who says that they're going to give me some sweets, then she'll murder me herself. But what I wants to know is, how can she murder me herself, when the nasty people has murdered me first?

Well, Mrs Jones-Evans aren't very nice to us kids, is she. But is she one of them nasty people who wants to murder me? She's always saying that she'd like to murder Johnny Merry. But all the grown-ups down our street says that they wants to murder Johnny Merry, and some of the grown-ups down the Hill says it as well, and down the other streets and down town as well. There's hundreds and hundreds of grown-ups who says that they wants to murder Johnny Merry. But he don't care, because when they says that to him he always tells them that he'd like to murder them, as well.

Once, we was down town and a man told us off for sitting on his doorstep. He told us, "Sod off, you lot. You scruffy little buggers makes the place look untidy."

We was only having a rest because it was hot and we'd been playing for a long time and we was tired. Johnny Merry put on his posh voice and told him, "Do you know who I am, my good man?"

"No, I don't, and I don't bloody care, neither," the man shouted. "Just sod off!"

"If you shout at me, my good man, I shall fetch the coppers to you," Johnny Merry told him in his posh voice.

"If you don't sod off this minute, you won't be able to fetch any bloody coppers because I'll murder you, you cheeky little bleeder. Now just sod off!"

And we went off and he slammed the door ever so loud.

Then we went back and Johnny Merry knocked on the door, and when the man come Johnny Merry said in his posh voice, "Can I have a drink of water, my good man?"

The man come roaring after us, and we all run, and the man picked up a stone and chucked it at us, and the stone hit a window and broke it, and the woman come running out of the house skreeking, and the man just stood there skreeking, "I'll murder you, you little bleeder. I'll murder you!"

We didn't half laugh when we run away. But see, it's true, aren't it? There's hundreds and hundreds of grown-ups who wants to murder Johnny Merry.

Well, I went with Mrs Jones-Evans to get a sweet, she wouldn't let Johnny Merry come though. But I wouldn't go inside her house in case she wanted to murder me, so she brought the sweet out to me. It was only a barley sugar, and I wished it was a chocolate. Then she asked me, "You know that little bunny-rabbit of yours, that ate the valuable ring, what colour is its fur?"

At first I didn't know what she was on about. Then I remembered what my Mam had said to Uncle Sid about saying that one of the rabbits had ate a precious ring. But I remembered as well what my Mam had told me to say. So I told Mrs Jones-Evans, "I don't know nothing about nothing."

She made me stay there for ages, and she give me some more barley sugars and she kept on asking me what colour the rabbit's fur was, and I kept on telling her, "I don't know nothing about nothing."

In the end she let me go, and when she went back into her house I heard her shouting to Mr Jones-Evans, "It must be true, Idris, because that scruffy little monster has obviously been sworn to secrecy by that awful mother of his."

I run home and I told my Mam what Mrs Jones-Evans

had said about me and her, and I thought that my Mam would go round to her house and tell her off about it, but my Mam only hugged herself and laughed all joyful. Then she hugged me, and kissed me, and told me, "You keep up the good work, Specs."

I don't like it when my Mam kisses me, because she makes my face all wet and sticky, and her breath smells of onions.

Chapter Thirty-Two

I was talking to some Jerries yesterday. Yeah, it's true! There was two of them down our street, and they had bikes as well. They was wearing brown battledress with big yellow round pieces on the back, and they was talking in English to us kids.

You know Miss Freeman's lilac tree in her back garden, well the Jerries told us that when they was living in Berlin there was a street there with trees all down it. One of the Jerries wrote on a piece of paper, 'Unter Den Linden' and said that was the name of the street. But I don't know what that means.

Anyway, one of the Jerries had a pecking chickens with him, and he said that he'd give it to us for a packet of fags. Have you seen the pecking chickens? It's ever so good. It's like a ping pong bat with wooden chickens on it, and there's bits of wood on string hanging down underneath it, and when you swings the strings the chickens starts to peck at the bat, just like real chickens does. Uncle Harold says that all the Jerries makes them. He says that hundreds of years ago when we was fighting Napoleon, the French prisoners used to make them as well.

Well, none of us kids had a packet of fags, but there was a big kid there called Billy who lives down town, and he told the Jerries, "Wait here, I'll get you some fags."

Me and Johnny Merry followed him when he went up the street, and he went to a shop round the corner called Miss Wilkes.

Miss Wilkes is ever so old, you know. She's all wrinkly, and she's got white whiskers and she's deaf. She can't hear the bell when you opens the door, so what she's got is a big coloured paper ball on a long string and when you opens the door the ball bounces up and down and she sees it and she comes out from the back room to see what you wants. My Mam sends me to Miss Wilkes to get her Woodbines six times a week. But she always sends me when I'm playing and it makes me ever so mad. She sent me one day and she give me a two shilling piece to get the fags with, and I was so mad I chucked it on the ground, and it rolled down the drain, and got lost. I wasn't half fritted when I lost it, because I knew that my Mam would give me a tanning when she found out what I did. And I started to cry, and Johnny Merry come along and asked me why I was crying, and I told him. So he went and pinched two shillings from his big sister Doreen's bag for me so I could get my Mam's Woodbines from Miss Wilkes. That was kind of him, wasn't it?

Well, the big kid, Billy, went to Miss Wilkes' shop, and what he did was to open the door just a little crack, and he got a stick and he pushed it into the paper ball, so that it couldn't move, and then he unhooked the string and snuck into the shop, and when he come out he had a packet of fags in his hand.

Then he saw us, and he told us, "If you says anything, I'll come and beat you up."

234

I was fritted of him, but Johnny Merry told him, "That's what you thinks. My dad's a copper and I'm going to tell him about you. And if you tries to beat me up, my Dad'll put you in jail."

Well, this big kid don't live in our street, so he don't know that Johnny Merry is telling him fibs, and he looked a bit fritted, and then Johny Merry told him, "Come on, just you try and beat us up. Come on, just try it! My Dad'll have you in jail in two shakes of a monkey's tail."

Then the big kid said to Johnny Merry, "I was only joking."

And Johnny Merry said, "I aren't joking. I knows where you lives, and I'm going to tell my Dad on you. You'll go to jail when I does that. You better give me them fags or I'll tell my Dad on you."

And the big kid got fritted then, and he chucked the fags down on the ground and he run away. And Johny Merry picked up the fags and put them in his pocket.

"What's you going to do with them?" I asked him, and Johnny Merry told me, "Come on. We'll get them pecking chickens off the Jerries."

So that's what we did. But after a bit the chickens broke, so they wasn't any good any more, and we give them to Letty Dobbs.

What I can't understand is, that all the grown-ups used to say that the Jerries was all horrible and should all be dead, but now when the Jerry prisoners comes down our street the Hostel girls talks to them and laughs and jokes with them, and some of the grown-ups does as well. Mrs Masters gives the Jerries cups of tea, and when I asked her why she gives them cups of tea, she just looked all sad and told me, "The lads are some poor mother's sons, Specs."

But I suppose it's alright for Mrs Masters to give the Jerries cups of tea, arn't it, because her Henry is fighting the Japs and not the Jerries.

Mrs Savin don't give them cups of tea though, because her Colin was killed in the desert, and Frankie is still fighting the Jerries, arn't he. But one day I heard her telling my Mam, "I don't have any hate for these poor young sods, Effie. They had to go and fight, just like my Colin and Frankie did. Only I can't forget what happened to my Colin, and until my Frankie comes home safe and sound I'll never be able to talk civil to any Jerry."

I heard my Mam telling Hilda about what Mrs Savin had said, and then my Mam said, "Does you know young Sheila Hancock from down Morton Road?"

And Hilda said, "Does you mean her that went into the Land Army? The big fat 'un that looks like a Paddy Navvy?"

"That's her," my Mam said. "She went to work on a farm down Evesham way and there was some Jerry prisoners working on the farm, and guess what? Young Sheila's having a babby from one of them. Talk about collaborating with the enemy!"

Hilda just laughed and told her, "Well, so long as she don't name the babby Adolf, who'll be able to tell the difference between him and an English babby?"

"Suppose it's a girl?" my Mam said, and Hilda told her, "Well, in that case, Sheila had better not name it Eva Braun."

And then they both laughed. But I don't know why. Who is Eva Braun anyway? Is she on the pictures? There was a good serial at the Gaumont Club last Saturday morning. It was 'Flash Gordon and the Emperor Ming'.

236

Flash Gordon crashed his spaceship right into the Emperor Ming's palace. I bet if Flash Gordon was on our side we'd have beat the Jerries and the Japs as easy as winking. Flash Gordon's ever so tough, you know, and he's the best fighter in the Universe.

Chapter Thirty-Three

All the neighbours was whispering down the entry when I come back from school today, and Clara the Clarion said when she saw me, "Has your Mam found her ring yet, Specs?"

"I don't know nothing about nothing," I told her, and they all looked at each other then, and nodded all wisely, and Mrs Masters said, "Come on, Chucky Face, you can tell me, can't you! Has your Mam found that ring yet?"

"I don't know nothing about nothing," I told her.

"See?" Clara the Clarion was looking all triumphant. "Didn't I tell you? That little bleeder has been sworn to secrecy. And I'll tell you summat else, as well. I saw Sidney Tompkins digging in the garden at two o'clock this morning. I had to get up to empty my old man's po because he's got that bladder trouble again, you know, and he fills the bloody thing three times a night. Well, it was bright as day in the moonlight and I saw Sidney Tompkins digging in the garden just as clear as I can see you now. And it's as plain as the nose on your face what he was digging for, arn't it?"

"Of course it is, Clara." Mrs Masters was grinning all over her face. "He was digging for victory, wasn't he?"

That's summat that the posters has got on them, you

know. 'Dig for Victory.' And they shows a picture of a big boot pushing a spade down into the dirt, and there's lots of vegetables and potatoes with funny faces and that coming up out of the ground.

"Dig for Victory? That lazy idle bugger?" Clara the Clarion sounded all scornful. "No wonder that bloody victory is such a long time coming then, if we'm waiting for bloody Sidney Tompkins to dig for it."

"What was he digging for then, Clara?" one of the other women asked her.

"He was digging them rabbits out of their burrows, and he was going to kill them and slit them open to find out which one had ate that bloody ring. It's like I told you it said in that letter. One of them rabbits has ate a valuable ring that's worth thousands of pounds."

Mrs Masters looked all stern at me. "Now then, Specs, is that what your Uncle Sid was doing? Digging out them rabbits to kill them?"

"I don't know nothing about nothing," I told her.

I saw a film at the pictures with a man in it who the Jerries had caught spying, and they was beating him up and asking him who the other spies were, and he kept on telling them, "I don't know nothing about nothing." And then some other men come who killed the Jerries and set him free, and he went back and his sweetheart said that she loved him because he was so brave and he hadn't told the Jerries nothing about nothing.

I wonder if Rita Spencer will like me because I'm being so brave and telling everybody, "I don't know nothing about nothing."

But I know why Uncle Sid was digging in the garden last night. It's because when my Mam drownded the last

240

lot of kittens she buried them in Uncle Sid's best sock down the garden. And what he was doing was digging holes to see if he could find the sock again, because he arn't got any socks left now, and he arn't got any clothing coupons to get some more with because my Mam give the coupons to Esther Lee, didn't she, to save us kids from that ghost.

I got a hole in the bottom of my boot as well, and my Mam says that she can't get me any more for ages because she can't afford it, so what she does is to cut pieces of cardboard the same shape as my foot and puts that in the boot to cover the hole up with. It's alright when it arn't raining, because then the cardboard lasts all day, but when it rains it's no good, because the cardboard gets all wet and soggy straight away and falls to bits.

Johnny Merry's big sister, Doreen, arn't got any more nylon stockings neither, now that her boyfriend arn't a Blackie Yank and is only a Pole. So what she does is to rub gravy browning on her legs, and then she gets a black pencil and draws long lines down the backs of her legs so that it looks like she's wearing nylon stockings.

Uncle Sid says that if she'd gone back to America with that Blackie then she'd have had to rub gravy browning all over her, so that people would think she was a Blackie herself, because if they didn't think that she was a Blackie, then she wouldn't be able to go and work in the fields picking cotton like all the other Blackies does.

Well, Clara the Clarion told the other women, "I'll tell you what, girls, I'm going to lay out some snares in my bloody patch right away. There's at least a dozen of them rabbits burrowing under my cabbages."

Just as she said that Johnny Merry come down the entry

to call for me, and Mrs Landers said, "Here·it comes, the bloody Pestilence. They ought to make this little sod keep on shouting 'Unclean' and carry a bell to ring so that decent folks knows when he's coming near."

Johnny Merry heard her say that, and ever so quick he put on his posh voice and told her, "I'm not going to start doing what you has to do when you goes down town, my good woman."

Mrs Masters laughed when he said that, but Mrs Landers looked daggers at him, but Johnny Merry don't care about her, because she can't run fast enough to catch him.

When we went down the street to see if there was any adventures, there was a lot of men and women running about all over the place chasing the rabbits. They was getting all excited and shouting and trampling down everything, and fighting with each other whenever one of them copped a rabbit.

Then we saw Fred Ferret coming up the street, with his sack bag over his shoulder, and the Stargazer was with him carrying the nets and talking to the sky.

Fred Ferret arn't his real name, but it's what everybody calls him because he lives in a house full of ferrets, and he likes ferrets so much that he's always got some in his pockets and under his cap. He's only ever so little and he wears a great big cap that hangs down to his ears and he wears big leather gaiters up to his knees and a big loose coat down to his feet that's got lots and lots of pockets inside and out.

My Mam says that he looks more like a ferret than a ferret does and she says that he's the craftiest poacher that's ever been born. His dog is named Edgar Ferret, and it runs about all over the town seeing what it can pinch.

All the butchers hates Edgar Ferret because he pinches the meat and sausages and pork pies from out of their shops and runs off with them to bring them to Fred Ferret.

Mr Allwood down our street used to keep pigeons in a great big loft in his back yard, you know, but my Mam says that Fred Ferret poached all of Mr Allwood's pigeons and that's why the loft is empty now. My Mam says that Mr Allwood goes and sits in the loft when he comes back from the pub drunk, and sings sad laments for his missing pigeons. He likes to sing, 'Danny Boy' the best, because that's all sad and sorrowful. She says that Mr Allwood loved them pigeons more than he loved his missus, but she says that that's understandable when you looks at the state of his missus.

"Where are you going, Fred?" we asked Fred Ferret. "Can we come?"

"Ahrrr," he told us.

That's the only thing that Fred Ferret says, you know, is "Ahrrr." But he says it in all different ways so we knows what he means.

Then he told us, "Ahrrr Ahrrr Jones-Evans. Ahrrrr, Ahrr, Ahrrrr Stargazer Ahrr."

That means that he's going to Mr Jones-Evans' house to catch the rabbits with his ferrets and nets. And we can help Stargazer hold the nets to catch the rabbits in.

"I'm sick of listening to your bloody claptrap," Stargazer was telling the sky, and he was getting all mad at it, I could tell.

Stargazer is all tall and skinny and he always wears his Mam's old pink coat, and a scout's hat that the brim dangles down on because it's all torn. And round his neck he wears a fox fur with a real head and glass eyes. Nobody knows how old Stargazer is, or why he only talks to the sky and not to people.

"Ah, you're changing your tune now, aren't you?" he said to the sky. "You're becoming a bit more friendly, aren't you? Well, I'm not a chap to hold a grudge. I'm prepared to meet you halfway on this point."

He never looks at the ground, you know, and I don't know how he can find his way about, because he never looks anywhere except at the sky.

Johnny Merry says that he was in Stargazer's house one day when Stargazer's Mam was giving him his dinner. Johnny Merry says that Stargazer was standing in the corner of the room talking to the ceiling, and that his Mam had to get on a ladder so that she could put the food into his mouth and give him some tea to drink. Johnny Merry says that she poured the tea straight from the pot down Stargazer's throat while he was talking to the ceiling and it just went straight down his gullet and he never stopped talking for a minute, not when he was eating his chips nor his piece of bread and jam neither.

Uncle Harold told me one day, "Do you know, Specs, that the Stargazer and myself have got a lot in common. Like myself, he also was a brilliant scholar and he was expected to take the highest academic honours that this country can bestow. But tragically his brain became overstrained with all the knowledge it contained and that he was racing to cram into it, and he had a mental breakdown. And that's why now he can only talk drivel."

"Well, that's summat you and he have certainly got in common anyway, Harold," Uncle Sid said all sarcastic-like. "But I arn't so sure about the first part of what you're claiming."

When we went into Mr Jones-Evans' back garden Fred Ferret told Edgar Ferret, "Ahrr Ahrr Ahrrrrr, Edgar."

That means, "Go and find the rabbit holes, Edgar."

And Edgar run about snuffling and digging into different places, and then he come back and barked at Fred, and Fred told us, "Edgar Ahrrr Ahrrrr Ahrrr Stargazer Ahrrr Ahrr Ahrrr Ahrrr."

That means, "Edgar says that there are eighty-three rabbits beneath this piece of land, and the best place to start is at the top of the grass there. So you two go with Stargazer and spread them nets across them holes, and I'll let the ferrets get at them."

"Ahrrr Ahrrr, Fred," Johnny Merry told him, and Fred looked a bit close at him then, but Johnny Merry kept his face straight, and we went and spread the nets like he told us. Us two at one end and Stargazer at the other.

"I cannot really whole-heartedly accept the doctrine of Transubstantiation," Stargazer was telling the sky, "although I must admit that your argument in its favour carries some telling points of quite considerable authority."

Fred Ferret emptied his sack out and there was hundreds and hundreds of ferrets come out of it, and he was picking them up and shoving them down the different rabbit holes, and then we saw Aubrey the posh kid coming down the garden path, and he was walking hand in hand with Rita Spencer!!!!.

"Heyyaa Rita," I said to her, but she just looked at me, and pulled a face and then turned her back on me. And Aubrey grinned all triumphant. He knows that Rita Spencer is my sweetheart, you know. He's horrible, Aubrey is. I don't like him. I was going to scrag him, but then the rabbits started to come running out of their holes and bouncing against the net, and quick as a flash Fred Ferret was grabbing them and putting them into his sack bags, and the bags was jumping all over the garden.

Aubrey the posh kid stared all haughty at Fred Ferret. "I say, you there!" he said to Fred. "My mother wants you to kill those rabbits and look inside their stomachs. One of them has eaten a very valuable ring that my mother had given to her by a Maharajah when she was a small child."

"Ahhrrr Ahrr, Ahhrrr Ahr," Fred told him.

That means, "Sod off you little toe-rag! I'm taking these rabbits back home with me."

Only Aubrey can't speak Fred's language, you see, so he didn't know what Fred saying to him and he told him ever so snotty, "I'm going to tell my mother about you for stealing our rabbits. And she'll fetch a policeman to you."

Fred looked daggers at him then, and he took a great big ferret out from under his cap and he whispered to it and pointed at Aubrey, and the ferret stared ever so evil at Aubrey, and it started to gnash its teeth together and to squeal and squeak, and Fred put the ferret on the ground and shouted, "Ahrr Ahrrr Ahrrr!"

That means, "Get that little toe-rag and tear him into shreds."

And the ferret went running at Aubrey, and Aubrey and Rita Spencer both started skreeking and run up into the house.

Mrs Jones-Evans come roaring out and when the ferret went towards her she just kicked it up in the air, and it went flying over the bushes. Then she come running down the

246

path and me and Johnny Merry was laughing and waiting to see what she'd do to Fred Ferret and Stargazer.

Stargazer just stood there talking to the sky, and he was giggling, "I do find your arguments facile and specious, Old Boy. You must forgive my levity, but I cannot help but be amused."

Mrs Jones-Evans run right past him and then she run right past Fred Ferret and Edgar Ferret and she grabbed me and Johnny Merry and started shaking us and skreeking, "I'll teach you two monsters to frighten those dear children with that savage beast."

"We aren't done nothing!" I told her, but she banged my head against Johnny Merry's head and skreeked, "My darling son has told me everything. And his sweet little friend Rita confirmed the truth of what he said. You two are the evillest little monsters I've ever come across."

And she kept on shaking us 'til our teeth was rattling, and knocking our heads together 'til they was banging like drums.

"Tell her, Fred," Johnny Merry shouted at him. "Tell her what you did with your ferret. Tell her that it wasn't us."

"Yeah, tell her, Fred." I shouted as well.

But all Fred did was to grin and say, "Ahrr Ahrrr Ahrrr."

That means, "You're on your own in this one, lads."

And he picked up the sacks of rabbits and ferrets and him and Edgar went away, and Stargazer picked up the nets and he followed him and we shouted to Stargazer, "Tell her, Stargazer."

But he was still talking to the sky, and telling it, "I really must refer you to the conclusion reached at the Convocation of Prague in 1847, when Sponderhuntz totally disclaimed any responsibility for the Theory of the Subdivision of the Incarnate Soul."

Then Johnny Merry did his fit.

He went all slack and held his breath and his face went all red and purple and then he bubbled his spit out from his mouth.

Mrs Jones-Evans skreeked and dropped him, and he lay on the ground on his back and did his flopping about. And Mrs Jones-Evans went running up the garden skreeking, "Oh my God! Oh my God! Idris! Idris! Come quick, Idris! Oh my God!"

And me and Johnny Merry run away down the garden and got through a hole in the hedge. We knew the hole was there because we made it ages ago so that we could get in and scrump her raspberries and her gussgogs. She's horrible, Mrs Jones-Evans is, and Aubrey is horrible as well. I don't like them.

"What shall we do now?" I asked Johnny Merry, when we'd run away from the garden.

"Let's go and roll boulders down Mrs Berrod's entry," he said. "We arn't been chased by her for ages."

So that's what we did.

It was smashing fun, she come running out with a big long poker in her hand and she chased us all up the street, shrieking, "I'll bloody well flay you, you little buggers."

We didn't half laugh.

Then I went home for a piece of jam, and all the neighbours was in our house, and they was all laughing and crying and being joyful. And when I asked my Mam what was going on, she picked me up and kissed me, and made my face all wet and sticky, and she told me, "The war's over, Specs. The man on the wireless has just said that the Jerries has surrendered. It's all over. Everything's going to be different now."

But I don't feel all joyful. Because I don't want everything to be different. Because I likes everything just as it is. It arn't fair, is it. Us kids never has a say in what things are going to be, does we. It just arn't fair."